M000032236

Cover Illustration by
Bruce Bealmear

Editor
Samantha Adams

Editorial Assistant
Patricia Thompson

ACKNOWLEDGMENTS

This story is based in part on *The Lovewell Family*, compiled by Gloria G. Lovewell of Lakeside, Oregon. The history was used with her permission. Much of her information is based on notes kept by Orel Jane Lovewell. Also used were family records of Mrs. Walter Poole, a granddaughter; *What Price White Rock*, by Harry E. Ross, and other sources. Indian history and information is based in part on the book, *Wild Life on the Plains and Horrors of Indian Warfare*, co-authored by General George A. Custer.

Many thanks to my wife, Irene, who patiently read proofs, and to Dr. Dwight Marsh, professor of advanced English Composition at Hastings College, for his able assistance in putting this story together in its most correct and readable form.

Lovewell family gathering, May 1914, left to right: Back Row - William Frank Lovewell, Grant Lovewell (holding Freida Lovewell) Pansy (Lovewell) Wirth, (unknown) Steve Lovewell, Edna Lovewell, Mrs. Hutchins, Mary (Lovewell) Stofer, Ben Stofer. Middle Row Standing - Lulu Lovewell, Cora Del Lovewell, Miss Wirth, Ethel Stofer, Orel Lovewell. Seated - Thomas Lovewell, Orel Jane Lovewell, Front Row - Bennie Stofer, Frankie (James Franklin) Lovewell, young Tom Lovewell, Leonard Lovewell, Wilma Lovewell, Daisy Lovewell, Dolly Lovewell, (the next two are unknown), Pansy Stofer.

ONE

Thomas Lovewell studied the rich, black dirt that dribbled through his fingers. It was the kind of soil any farmer would like to see and feel. He had just dug a hole three feet deep and this bottom soil was just as black as the first shovelful. It was there for the taking, and it was so deep it would last forever.

The tall switch, Indian and bluestem grasses he pushed aside to find the soil told him the land was rich and productive. The grass stood as tall as his six-foot frame, although some of it had matted down under winter snows. It was spring, and the new grass stems were poking through the sod. The roots, tenacious and hard to cut, extended beyond his three-foot hole.

Catfish, bass and other fish jumped in the clear stream nearby that flowed near the south side of the wide valley. He couldn't see far for the tall grass, so he climbed the hill to the south for a better view. To the southwest rose a round mound with protruding white and yellow sandstone. The valley, which Tom dubbed White Rock, stretched some ten miles west and disappeared in the hills. Tall, straight cedar and pine trees stretched along the hillsides; a grove of tall cottonwoods snuggled in the valley to the east. All were just right for building homes, barns and corrals. Tom named the stream that flowed through the valley White Rock Creek. Cottonwood and black walnut trees flanked its banks, which were interspersed with wild cherry and plum thickets. Swollen by spring floods, the creek jumped its banks as it wiggled along the south side of the

4

valley. It flowed eastward into the Republican River, which swung south from Nebraska Territory into Kansas Territory.

Surely the Garden of Eden—or maybe even heaven—couldn't have been more wonderful than this. As Tom gazed out on the valley he made his mind up: someday this would be his home. He was dreaming already of the cattle he would raise in the hills to the south and the corn and cattle feed he would grow in the valley. After making up with Nancy, his wife of a few years, he would bring her and their two daughters to this valley.

But first he would investigate the valley further. With his long muzzle-loading rifle under his arm and his revolver tucked in his belt, he swung up the valley. He covered the land quickly with his long stride. Early explorers, convinced the region would never be fit for agriculture, had named it the Great American Desert. But the raindrops sparkling from the leaves and grass convinced Tom the rainfall was adequate for crops and grass. Small game, such as prairie chicken and grouse, barely bothered to fly out of his way as he walked along. A raccoon chattered from the top of a cottonwood tree. Larger game—deer, elk and antelope—ran ahead of him as he walked westward. Their young scampered around and played tag. The plentiful game, including the buffalo he saw in the distant hills, would be his commissary. With meat on the hoof, grass for his future cattle herd, running water for his home and livestock and rich soil to furnish grains and garden stuff, what could be better?

Tom went back to his three yoke of oxen, watered them in the river and fixed himself a meal of elk steak and biscuits in his Dutch oven. He could see the wagon train he had joined camped to the east. The boss had decreed a day of rest, hence his chance to study the valley. He liked to camp away from the train to give his oxen the best forage. Their bulging sides and contented cud-chewing convinced him it was worth the risk. They would need plenty of good grass for the long trek to Denver, where he planned to sell the wagonload of miner supplies he had brought from Illinois.

The wagon boss warned him about crossing the Republican River. "The Indians think they have a treaty that limits white settlers to land east of this river," he said. But white men had a habit of ignoring treaties with

Indians. Tom would do likewise when he returned from the gold fields with his fortune. Of course he had to get there first, and that might be much more of a challenge than he and many others thought. The Platte River road and the long trip across the plains to Denver stood between him and the gold fields that would end the poverty and hard times he had grown up with in Ohio.

That night under the wagon Tom slept fitfully as he dreamed of White Rock Valley and thought deeply of his past. Though he was only twenty-three, he felt as though he had lived through a lifetime of trouble and hardship.

TWO

It was after midnight on December 20, 1826. On the farm of Moody Bedell and Elizabeth Watkins Lovewell in Athens County, Ohio, Mrs. Lovewell had recovered from the birth of Thomas, their sixth son. The midwife had gone home. "Isn't he a beautiful child?" Mrs. Lovewell asked.

"He sure doesn't have your red hair," Bedell said. "It's as black as coal. He'll be tall and muscular—a big help on the farm. But it's going to be hard to feed one more mouth."

"We'll manage."

At daylight he left his wife to feed the small flock of sheep in the corral and milk the cow. He pulled shucks from the ears of corn in the shock, broke off a few ears and laid them aside. He fed the stalks to the cow and cut up two ears for her. Then he shelled off a few kernels for the sheep and spread them in the trough before shelling a few more ears for home use. They would be ground for corn mush and corn bread, the main items in their daily diet.

He wanted to leave some corn to take to market. The price was so low it was hardly worth the effort, but they needed cash for a few necessities such as salt and sugar. When Elizabeth was able she would again spin thread for clothes, spending hours at her spinning wheel while singing softly to little Thomas.

The nation was beset by hard times brought on by a depression. Families, including the Lovewells, had a hard time putting food on the table. Some farmers augmented their income with stills, which they used to convert grain into whiskey. The Lovewells would have no part of it.

"We will have no part of likker," Elizabeth said. "We'll make do with what we have—at least we have wool and warm clothing. We want our boys to grow up to be honest, law-abiding men who don't learn to drink whiskey before they are old enough to get married."

Bedell never let his boys forget that they came from good British stock. "Our ancestry reaches back to Scotland," he would tell them proudly, "and way before that. Our folks were among the first to settle in America. Your grandfather, Sergeant Zacheus fought in the War of Independence under Colonel Timothy Bedell. He admired him so much he named me after him."

***

One spring day, when Tom was nine, an aunt and uncle whom the boys detested came for a visit. They drove up in a fancy surrey with fringe all around the top, pulled by a high-stepping black team. Their aunt was dressed in stylish clothes, a luxury she could afford since she and her husband had no children.

The couple stayed for lunch. When the skimpy noon meal was over the boys ran out to play and talk about their rich relatives. "Who wants to be like 'em," Ebenezer snorted.

Tom went back to sit on the porch and listen to the conversation in the house. What he heard was not about the depression or the good old days; the couple was discussing the Lovewell's large family and whether Bedell and Elizabeth could continue to provide for them all. "They look like ragamuffins and they never get enough to eat," his uncle said.

"How about if we take Tom, bring him up and educate him for you?" his aunt asked.

Tom didn't wait to hear more. He ran out to play with his brothers. He would rather starve than go with his domineering aunt.

That night in bed, Tom told his brother Will about the conversation. "What can I do?"

"Run away," Will said as he rolled over and went to sleep.

"Now that doesn't seem like a bad idea," Tom thought. He waited until he heard his father's loud snoring, then placed a few clothes in a bag and sneaked out. He ran out back, across the field and through the woods,

8

aimlessly running east toward the Hocking River. Toward morning, exhausted, he found a secluded spot among some brush, laid his head on his bag and fell asleep. That night he walked until he came to the river.

The next morning Tom was hungrier than he had ever been at home. Looking for work, he approached a towboat headed upstream hauled by strong men pulling from towpaths along the river. Although it was still early morning, the sweat poured off the men's foreheads and ran down their faces. It was evident to Tom that this was not a boy's job.

Tom almost turned back, but the gnawing in his stomach combined with the thought of his aunt and uncle stopped him. He approached the boss, who was intently watching the boat to see that his men didn't gee or haw too much and hang the boat on a sandbar or protruding root or downed limb. He ignored the boy standing nearby, thinking it was early for the curious boys from town, who usually came later in the morning.

Tom nudged the boss, who looked at him. "What do you want?"

"How about a job."

The boss looked him over, noting his gaunt looks, ragged clothes and his size; Tom was large for his age. The boss spat a big wad from the cud in his mouth into the river, where it turned brown for a moment.

"Ya run away or somethin'?"

"I'm an orphan. I'm hungry and I need a job."

"Well, I'll give you a job but ya better do good. Ya don't look like you can handle it."

"I'm used to hard work. I can handle it, you'll see."

Tom worked hard to convince the boss he could handle his share of the work, but helping tow a boat up the river was too much for him. Soon he was all used up.

The workers cursed him roundly for not doing his share. "Why'd you hire that dang kid," one asked the boss.

The boat came back for another load. Tom knew he would be fired but it didn't matter. He was ready to surrender to his aunt and uncle when he saw his father hail the boss.

"Got a young lad on your crew?"

"This your son? He said he was an orphan."

"Why'd you leave, son," his father asked, putting an arm on his shoulder as they walked home.

"I just didn't want to live with those folks."

"Son, we never would have sent you to live with them without talking it over with you first, and you wouldn't have had to go if you didn't want to. You could have learned a lot and maybe one of us might have amounted to something. But it's your decision. I don't see how you stood that work."

"It was awful."

When Tom was twelve he went to work again for the same boss, towing boats up the Hocking River. This time he stayed with the job, growing strong in the process. He quit when he was sixteen and headed out on his own for good.

***

Tom's first job after leaving home was on an Ohio River boat. He also began visiting Nancy Davis, of whom he was now more than just fond. Her father was a minister, and they had attended Sunday School together. Sometimes he walked her home; other times they sat on her porch for a while before he ran home. All the girls began to notice the tall young man with the dark hair and handsome figure, but at the parties they attended, Tom saw to it that Nancy was his partner as often as possible.

"How about a picnic?" Nancy suggested one day. Together they fixed a basket of sandwiches, apple pie and a jug of water and walked down the hill to a grassy spot along the creek. Tom threw stones across the water. Nancy giggled when one of the pebbles skipped across the water, hit a tree on the other side and scared a rabbit that dashed into the woods. A blue jay scolded from its perch high in the tree. A robin sang spiritedly and a cow mooed for her calf as she stopped at the creek for a drink. The sun shown brightly and the grass was warm.

"It's a great day to be alive," Tom said. "It's fun just to sit here with you and soak up the sunshine." Nancy sat back against a tree and nodded in agreement. Tom stretched out on the fresh-smelling green grass. Neither said much as they relaxed and enjoyed each other's company. Tom looked at Nancy and suddenly realized she was not the same spindly legged girl who raced him to the fishing hole to be the first to hook a wriggly worm. Her sandy hair fell down in pretty ringlets around her full, beautiful face. She stood more than five feet tall, her slight build in full bloom. In other words, she was a woman.

Despite the perfect day, Tom and Nancy's budding relationship was clouded by his plans to seek his fortune elsewhere.

"When will you be back?" Nancy queried, touching his hand.

"Not until I have enough money to start farming and get married."

"And who are you going to marry," she prodded.

Tom squeezed her hand and hesitated. "You—if you'll have me."

Nancy leaned over and gave him a kiss. "Does that answer you question?" Her smile said it all.

Tom jumped up, pulled her to him and kissed her. "We must go or your folks will wonder what happened to us."

"Don't be gone too long," Nancy begged when he kissed her good-bye that evening.

The next day Tom boarded a boat headed down the Ohio River. At St. Louis he signed on as a roustabout on a boat hauling freight to New Orleans. The hard work built his muscles even more. His height and size didn't go unnoticed by other young men and he was frequently challenged to wrestle. He won a few and lost a few. His favorite technique was to wait for the challenger to come at him, crouch low, grab him by the legs and hoist him over his head. When his opponent lit, Tom bounced on him and pinned him to the ground. The stamina he gained would come in handy years later.

In New Orleans Tom and a buddy wandered from saloon to saloon. Tom had never drank before and the stuff tasted like running a rough wire down the throat. He gagged and pretended he liked it.

More intent on avoiding boredom than drinking, the two wandered on through the city. Eventually they happened upon a slave auction, where they saw black men, women and children being sold to the highest bidders. Since slavery was not as prominent in Ohio, the experience was a new and disturbing one for Tom.

Families were split: one woman sold as a good breeder, while a man sold as a good buck, capable of siring the husky boys and girls the trade demanded. It was the darkest side of slavery. Many plantations were good to their slaves and kept families together even when sold. But not all.

11

"They treat them just like cattle," Tom mumbled, thinking it better not to be heard.

A buyer overheard him. "Ya some kind of a slave lover?"

Tom turned and walked away from the auction. Later he said to his friend, "I'll never have anything to do with that business."

"Aw, they ain't people, they're just property," his buddy replied.

"They look like people and they act like people. As far as I'm concerned, they are people."

Tom told his friend a story his father had told of two blacks who escaped to the north, riding their master's saddle horses.

"They stopped at an anti-slavery farmhouse and asked for protection. The farmer kept them until the owners found them and tried to take them back. The farmer insisted they appear before a judge, who said they could have the horses but not the slaves. 'You say they are just property and have no rights, just like cattle. How do we know; maybe the horses picked up the slaves and carried them here. Take your horses and go,' he said.

"There'll be war over the slaves, and I'm going to be on the slaves' side," Tom added.

After a few days in New Orleans Tom's money began to run out. He couldn't find a boat going up river to work on, and he was getting hungry.

The nation was at war with Mexico, but recruiting volunteers for the army was not going well. Young men were uninterested in fighting a war in the wilds of Mexico, and recruiters were needed to sign up volunteers by any means necessary.

Walking back to Main Street, Tom saw a man setting up whiskey barrels on a platform and lining up rows of mugs. He motioned to Tom.

"Hey, young man, come here. Want a job? I'll pay you well."

"Doing what for how much?"

"Well, you see, I'm an army recruiter and we need soldiers. This is what we'll do: I'll make a patriotic speech and then I'll offer free drinks. When the men get drunk enough I'll sign them up and you steer them onto the ship there. If they are too drunk to walk it's your job to hustle them on board. I'll pay you one dollar per hour."

12

Whatever resistance Tom had to the work disappeared when he heard the wages, which equaled his pay for a whole day's work on the boat.

Unfortunately, the recruiting didn't go exactly as the officer had hoped. Potential recruits resisted more than expected; Tom had to carry some onto the ship. He helped get boys into the United States Army, but he didn't offer himself.

When it was over Tom had a coin belt filled with silver dollars, more money than he had seen in his whole life. He also had a sore chin from an unwilling recruit's blow and a sore shoulder from a slip on the gangplank.

It was time to go home. His family would be waiting and so would Nancy, he hoped.

Tom found sad news waiting for him at home. "Your mother died," his father told him when he returned. "Don't rightly know what her illness was, she died so quickly."

Tom recalled her beautiful long hair and the talks they had together. He also remembered her advice: "Be sure to learn to read and write and cipher." But he hadn't.

As his father prepared a simple meal of corn bread, bacon and coffee, they talked. "Your brother Solomon rigged up a covered wagon and joined thousands heading for Oregon Territory. Your sister married Tom Abbott and moved to Swan Creek, Illinois. The rest are scattered around.

"I stopped off in Arkansas," Tom said. "I saw your brother, who offered me a job. But he has slaves and I don't want anything to do with that, not that he wasn't good to them."

"Everyone says there will be war over slavery," Bedell answered. "In the meantime you can join me on the farm if you want to. And what about your other plans. You going to marry Nancy?"

"I'll let you know as soon as I see her. I have a little money now." Tom explained how he came into riches. His father frowned at the mention of liquor.

"I'll build a room onto your house and we'll raise a big family," Tom said.

13

When Tom went to see Nancy she welcomed him with a big hug and kiss.

"Still want to marry me?" Tom asked.

"Sure do."

"When?"

"Week from Sunday. My father can marry us. We won't have a big wedding," said Nancy.

"Suits me."

Tom helped his father with the corn tending. In the evenings he watched Nancy and her mother sew her beautiful white wedding gown. Nancy seldom looked up from her needle. "We have to hurry, you know," she would say.

Come Sunday Bedell Lovewell walked to the church. Tom splurged, renting a surrey that was almost as fancy as his aunt and uncle's years back. Tom bought himself a new black suit and new black boots. They were a stunning pair, Nancy in her white gown and white hat and Tom in his suit, though he was miserable in his stuffed shirt.

"You're the most beautiful bride in the whole world," Tom whispered as he walked with her into the church.

The churchyard filled with the buggies of relatives and neighbors. Still more walked to the little church, which filled to capacity.

Nancy's mother sat on a front pew between Nancy's brother, Daniel and sister, Orel Jane, who squirmed in their dress-up clothes. In a simple ceremony before the Reverend Vincent Davis Tom said "I do" in the right places.

After the crowd gathered to congratulate them, Tom lifted Nancy into the surrey pulled by two high-stepping blacks and took her for a ride in the country. They stopped at the creek bank where they had made their first vows. He pulled a blanket from the surrey and walked her to a grassy spot. The grass stained her dress green even though she held it high.

They stretched out on the blanket to enjoy the sunshine, watch the birds in the trees and listen to a cranky blue jay.

That night they slept in the guest room at the Davises, but the next morning they moved Nancy's belongings to the Lovewell farm. After dinner Tom went to the fields to get ready to harvest wheat and oats. With better prices and good crops, their future looked bright. But Nancy could see that Tom was restless.

Every day wagons, pulled by oxen, mules or horses rolled by, headed for Oregon. The exodus to the "promised land" was a frequent topic of conversation at the local store. Not much consideration was given to the fact that it would take all summer and then some to get there via the Oregon Trail.

***

One day Bedell received a letter from his son, Solomon, extolling the beauty of the land out West and its promised riches. "I urge you and Tom to move out," he wrote.

"It's not for me," Tom's father said. "I'm too old for that."

"But you would like to go," Nancy said to Tom.

"I'm not sure."

As settlers continued to head west, Tom's restlessness grew. Three years passed, during which Nancy gave birth to two girls, Nancy Jane and Julaney. Nancy was a beautiful child, with Tom's black hair and Nancy's smile. Julaney's hair was sandy, like Nancy's.

Then, late in 1848, word came of gold found in California at Sutter's mill. "I know he wants to go, but I don't," Nancy told her father-in-law. "I really don't feel well. I don't know what's the matter."

Tom and Nancy argued over the move for hours and nearly separated over it. Though Tom stopped short of jumping on a wagon to California, he still had gold fever. When he learned that gold had been discovered in the Rocky Mountains near Denver, Tom could resist no longer. He bought three yoke of oxen and a freight wagon and loaded it with miner's supplies.

"I'll sell the supplies to the miners and we'll have money for that farm we want to buy," Tom promised Nancy.

"And you'll stay and hunt for gold," she snapped.

Tom left his father and family with Rhodia and Tom Abbott at Swan Creek, Illinois, and headed west.

"I sure wish you wouldn't go," Nancy cried. "I'll never see you again."

15

"I'll be back next year," he promised.

But Tom's plans changed, and one year turned to several. He crossed the Missouri River and joined a wagon train that would take him past the beautiful White Rock Valley. In Denver he learned that the rumors of gold there were merely a false alarm, Tom joined another wagon train, this time to California. There he sold his supplies and found gold, too. True to his anti-slavery convictions, he volunteered for service when the Civil War broke out, though to his disappointment he ended up battling western Indians instead of Southern rebels.

Nearly sixteen years after leaving home, Tom started for home.

THREE

Tom woke to find a doctor sitting next to his bed. "Where am I?" he asked. "I don't seem to recall much. What happened?" Tom propped himself on the edge of his bed and tried to shake off his dizziness.

"You're in Fort Kearny. It's good to see you awake. You've been delirious now for thirty days with typhoid fever. You were a very sick man, but it looks as if you may make it now," the doctor said.

"Do you remember getting off the stage and walking to Fort Gothenburg on the north side of the river west of here, the fort set up to protect the Mormon Trail?"

"Yeah. I remember that now. I seem to remember leaving there and walking here. Seems like the captain urged me to stay because the Indians were on the warpath."

"Well, after you left there that morning, the Indians fired flaming arrows over the stockade onto a haystack, setting it afire. When the men tried to fight their way out of the fort, the Indians killed them all. The fort burned to the ground."

"That's terrible. I should have stayed and helped them. I was sick when I left that fort but I didn't know what was wrong. Anyway, when can I leave?"

"You will have to stay and recuperate for at least a month, then you   can   go.

The good doctor came to see Tom every day. They sat and visited for some time. "Where did you serve the Cause," the doctor asked.

"On the west coast, fighting Indians. I left home in 1849 with a load of mining supplies to sell at Denver. When I got there they hadn't found gold yet and I couldn't sell the supplies.

17

"So I took the load to California. I found gold at the head of a river and got rich. We tried for gold in Death Valley too—my whole party nearly died of thirst. When I heard they needed men for the war, I joined the army; I saw slaves auctioned in New Orleans and I wanted to fight slavery. Because I was in California, I ended up fighting Indians who were harassing settlers. The army told us the South incited the Indians to fight, but I doubt it. They discharged me at Fort Churchill, Nevada, on February 2. That's when I started for home."

***

After a few weeks of recuperation Tom left for Fort Riley, with plans to stop in White Rock Valley on the way. He walked, taking his rifle and carrying a few supplies on his back. Sleeping at secluded spots in the daytime and traveling at night, he finally arrived at Spring Ranch, Nebraska, a popular road ranch directly north of the White Rock Valley.

Tom traveled cautiously, and with good reason. The commanding officer at Fort Kearny told him how Indian tribes, resenting the invasion of their lands, had banded together to make war with the white man. The Indians began with sporadic attacks on lone wagons traveling the Platte Valley Road. The initial assaults were random and unplanned, but by 1864 they seemed well organized. They attacked road ranches all across Nebraska with remarkable success, killing many of the owners and their families. Soldiers from Forts McPherson and Kearny were sent out to subdue the Indians and assist the surprised owners, who mistakenly thought they were getting along quite well with the tribes.

From Spring Ranch, which he remembered so well as his jumping off spot for the west, Tom turned south to White Rock Valley. It was as beautiful as ever: the trees, the game, the abundant tall grass. Approaching the creek he saw what looked like a log house on the north side. Could it be that someone beat him to the valley? He crossed and examined it. It was deserted, though it showed signs of recent habitation. It was about ten by twelve feet, with a fireplace in one end. Firewood was stacked outside; old newspapers were strewn inside. There was an old iron bedstead in the corner. From the iron kettle hanging in the fireplace and the homemade shelf adorned with knickknacks, Tom gathered that the cabin had been a family home. No evidence remained telling who the newcomers might have been—no scraps of paper, no old letters. Outside, the sod was furrowed, but unplanted; whoever lived here must have left in a hurry. Tom wondered: were Indians on their tail?

Tom decided not to start a wood fire or stay in the cabin, though the bedstead was tempting. Instead he walked up the creek to a cottonwood grove, dined on cold meat and found a secluded spot for the day. Before resting he scanned the hills and the valley for signs of Indians.

The next night he followed the Republican River south toward Fort Riley. The old Overland Trail was still lined with pioneers, many of whom would homestead in the Rocky Mountains or on the high plains rather than going all the way to Oregon or California.

At the fort the medical officer declared Tom "fit as a fiddle." The general in charge offered him a job leading new settlers into western Kansas and northern Nebraska.

Tom said "Maybe later. Right now I'm on my way to Illinois to see my family. I've been gone for almost sixteen years." They talked of White Rock Valley, where Tom told the general he wanted to settle with his family.

"Better not—not now anyway," the general warned. "The Indians are on the warpath. They say stay east of the river. They have killed many settlers and road ranch people and scared the rest out. One family settled there in 1862 but left."

Thanking the general for his information and advice, Tom headed for Swan Creek, Illinois, to look up the family he hadn't seen for so long.

When he reached Swan Creek, Tom was disappointed to learn that his wife and father had died. His daughters were gone too, they had been adopted and were no longer in the area. Heartbroken, Tom quickly moved on to Keokuk, where he was told he would find his sister Rhodia and her husband, Tom.

As he entered Keokuk, Tom could see a livery barn and blacksmith shop at the end of Main Street with the sign "ABBOTT" hung overhead in bold letters. Inside the wide door the red coals and rising white smoke of the forge were visible. Outside, in the shade of a spreading walnut tree, a man bent over the hind foot of a tall, black draft horse. Holding the foot, he raised his hammer to drive in the first nail.

Sturdy homes, such as one might expect in a small farming community, spread out from the short Main Street. Stores essential to a rural community—clothing, food, a barbershop and a small hotel—some painted bright colors, lined either side of the street. Hitching rails were lined with buggies, wagons and shoppers' carriages. A half-dozen men lounged on a bench in front of the saloon, while a hazy dust rose from the dirt street. Ships were busy at the nearby port unloading store supplies and goods. Grain was being loaded for shipment south.

A few covered wagons moved slowly through town. These were late starters from back East who would have to winter somewhere along the way if they were going to California or Oregon. They headed west, probably for a frontier settlement or perhaps eastern Kansas. Some were pulled by heavy draft teams, most by oxen, a few by mules. Children ran beside the wagons, laughing and running back and forth. Mothers yelled at them to be careful not to fall beneath a wagon wheel. Tom shuddered, remembering children being killed when they fell beneath a heavily loaded wagon during his earlier trip west.

The wagons and families reminded Tom of his lost dream of settling in White Rock Valley with his family. He stood staring empty-eyed as the last wagon disappeared from town. His reveries were interrupted by the man with the horseshoe.

"What can I do for you?" the man asked as he approached.

"I'm looking for Rhodia Abbott," Tom replied.

"And who're you?"

"I'm her brother, Tom."

"Well, I'll be darned," he dropped the horse's foot so quickly that the animal nearly stomped on his foot as it snorted and jumped sideways.

They shook hands and visited for a while. There was so much news to catch up on. "You better get up and see your sister. Ours is the white house well past the end of Main Street with a verandah in front," Abbott added.

As Tom walked past the end of Main Street he passed a white schoolhouse. Children of all ages played in the schoolyard as the teacher stood by watching. She was slim and tall with dark hair and a beautiful

20

face that was somehow familiar. She reminded him of Nancy. He waved to her but she didn't wave back.

When Tom finally reached his sister's house, Rhodia recognized him as soon as she opened the door.

"Oh, Tom," was all she could say as she threw her arms about him. "I'm surprised that I knew you behind your black beard and long hair."

She plied him with questions as she fed him coffee and sandwiches. "Why didn't you write?"

"Well, you know I spent only nine days in school. I have learned to read and write a little since then, but I still don't do it well."

Rhodia caught Tom up on everything that had happened during his absence. "Our brothers fought on different sides in the Civil War. Ebenezer joined the South and we haven't heard from him since. We learned that Alfred contracted typhoid fever while his company was camped at Vicksburg. Trying to cool his fever he walked into the Mississippi River and drowned. His body was never recovered. Christian was killed during the war, but I don't know where. The rest of our family is scattered, those who are left. And what about you? Did you end up fighting in the war?"

It took a while for Tom to tell her about his experiences during those sixteen years: the gold, the desert, joining the army in San Francisco. He also shared his memories of the beautiful White Rock Valley. "I was planning to take the family to a pretty valley I found in Kansas. I visited Solomon in Oregon but I couldn't give up the idea of this valley in Kansas. Now with Nancy gone I don't know what to do."

"You're welcome to stay here," Rhodia offered. "Even if you don't, you should probably go see Nancy's family. They still live here, you know. Nancy's sister Orel Jane is the local schoolteacher."

"I thought she looked familiar."

"She does resemble Nancy. She married Alfred W. Moore, but they divorced. Later he was killed during the War. Her parents live here, too, and she and her son, Emery Perry, live with them. Her brother Daniel followed his father into the ministry."

"I'll go over and visit the Davises right away and be back for supper. I appreciate you letting me stay here Rhodia," Tom said. "Maybe while I'm here I can help Tom around the barn."

Reluctantly, Tom went to visit the Davises. He knew they would ask why he hadn't kept in touch, and he would have a hard time answering.

Like Rhodia, the Davises recognized Tom in spite of his beard and long hair. They, too, were glad to see him, but as Tom had feared they asked why he didn't write. He tried to explain that he didn't know how to write, but he grudgingly admitted that he had not asked anyone else to correspond for him.

"We supposed you had been killed along the way in that wild country," Mary Davis said. "Nancy worried and grieved about you so much—she just knew you were killed by Indians. She was always poorly, especially after you left, but she kept in touch faithfully by writing us often. When she died, a family adopted the girls and moved away. Sure wish we knew where they are. They were such pretty girls; they would remind you of Nancy."

"I'm sorry I was gone so long," Tom said after recounting his experiences through the years. "It seemed just when I was preparing to come back something always came up. I signed up for the army when the president declared war, thinking I would be sent back here. I wanted to fight slavery; instead I spent the whole time fighting Indians out there."

Nancy's parents introduced Tom to Orel Jane when she came home later that afternoon. "You were just a little girl when I left," Tom said.

"Yes, I think I was six, but I do remember you. Nancy talked of you so much. She always said she feared she would never see you again."

Tom said good-bye to the Davises and returned to Rhodia and Tom's for supper. Thankful for his sister's generous offer to let him stay, Tom's thoughts turned to life without Nancy and his children.

***

Each day Tom went down to the livery stable and helped his brother-in-law: cleaning out stalls, hitching up teams for the doctor, even helping to shoe horses. Sometimes he was hired to drive the local doctor to tend a patient. As he drove past cornfields, turning brown as they ripened, Tom would reminisce about White Rock Valley. Someday corn

22

would ripen there, but Tom feared he would not be there to pick it. Without a family to settle with, he just didn't have the interest he once did. Sometimes he thought of starting a new family, maybe with Orel Jane, but his thoughts frightened him. Surely she would think twice about marrying a man who had already deserted one family.

Despite his reservations, Tom's interest in Orel Jane grew. He began walking her home from school in the afternoon, and she would wait if he was late. The ritual was developing into a habit, perhaps even a love affair, although neither of them dared talk of such things. Tom spent more and more of his evenings with her. "I remember so many bad things, my divorce, that awful war," she said one afternoon, "but being with you makes me happy. Why don't you stay for supper tonight?"

That evening Orel Jane's father, Vincent, said he was interested in becoming a circuit rider on the frontier. "There must be a great need for ministers out there."

"Yeah, there's a great need all right. The land is being settled fast," Tom encouraged him. "I fell in love with White Rock Valley in Kansas and was hoping to take Nancy and the girls there. The army offered me $100 a month to guide settlers to new settlements but I turned it down. I saved a lot of my gold so I didn't need the money—besides, I was anxious to get home."

"Well, if you're still interested, why don't we go out there together? You could show us how to survive in that country."

"I would if Orel Jane would marry me," Tom said, casting a sly look across the table, where Orel Jane sat listening with unusual interest. If she was caught off guard, her surprise lasted only a moment. She looked at her father, then at Tom. Finally she looked long at Tom and uttered a low "Yes."

If Tom was surprised he didn't show it much. He ducked his head for a moment then glanced up, hoping she meant it.

"Well, if that's settled, let's start making plans," Vincent said. "We can prepare this winter and leave early next spring. One thing troubles me though, Tom. Is this valley of yours dangerous? We don't want to go where we might get killed by Indians."

"It's still somewhat dangerous. But it is such a pretty valley. The soil is rich and there's ample timber for houses and barns. You can't imagine how beautiful it is."

The four stayed up late talking. Little Emery fell asleep on Mary's lap and she put him in his cradle. Vincent went to bed, and Mary followed quickly.

Orel Jane and Tom sat on the living room couch and he put his arm around her. They talked far into the night, most of the night, in fact, making plans. Tom had trouble convincing Orel Jane that White Rock was the place to go.

"I'm worried about the Indians. I don't want to shoot anyone and I don't want to be shot at," she said, grimacing.

"The Indians will soon be on reservations. The whole land is being settled now that we have the new homestead law. We can homestead 160 acres and take another 160 by planting forty acres of trees. And it is all free. You'll fall in love with the land. You can even be our first teacher."

He didn't sound too convincing. "Well, maybe," she answered, giving him a big kiss through his scratchy beard.

"We can go through Missouri and have my brother Daniel marry us," Orel Jane suggested. "Maybe they will go with us. But I don't believe he and my father will think much of the unsettled country that far west."

Toward morning, Tom kissed her fondly. "I'll love you just as much as I did Nancy. We'll have a big family and give each of them farms in the valley."

"And build churches and schools," Orel Jane added, "and I will be the first teacher."

"Sounds good to me," Tom said as he walked out. The sun was just peeking over the horizon. There was new bounce in his step as he walked down the dusty street. He even whistled a bit of "Oh! Susanna!"

"Hey, come back," Orel Jane yelled, "might as well stay for breakfast." A neighbor woman watching from her porch listened in, a shocked look on her face. She quickly stepped back and slammed the door hard.

24

Each evening Tom was back with Orel Jane and the Davises, planning for the trip west in the spring. Orel Jane wrote to Daniel asking him to perform the wedding ceremony, while Tom spent his days lining up two wagons and oxen. He also bought two plows that would be capable of breaking the tough sod of the valley. Orel Jane insisted on taking some of her furniture, such as a bedstead and dresser and all of her schoolbooks, especially her notebooks. With all their preparations the winter passed quickly. Soon it was spring.

***

One Saturday Orel Jane and Tom packed a lunch and took a long walk through the woods along the Mississippi River. Along the riverbank they spread their lunch on a cloth and enjoyed the warm, clear spring air. Tom again tossed pebbles across the water and watched them skip. Orel Jane leaned back against a tall oak and looked up at the sky pensively. Tom walked back, sat down and held her hand. "Just like Nancy and I used to do," he said. "Her memory is very real, but now my heart is with you."

"I was very fond of her too. She had consumption and was never well after you left. She told me of your good times together. I was envious, I think. She would be glad that I took her place." Neither wanted the day to end as they walked back home well after dark, holding hands.

Orel Jane received her answer from her brother. The wedding date was set for April 1, 1865, at Davis's church in Gentry County, Missouri. Daniel and Mary Davis would go west with Tom, Orel Jane and her parents. But he would not take a rifle and that worried Tom. Indians were constantly on the warpath, it seemed. The army was trying to move them onto reservations, such as those in Oklahoma, but it didn't appear as though they were having much success. Despite the fearsome reports, Tom was as determined as ever to homestead in White Rock Valley.

Vincent still worried about trouble with the Indians, but Tom tried to ease his fears. "Don't worry," he said with more confidence than he felt, "the army will take care of them."

"That doesn't jibe with all the horror stories we hear from travelers coming this way."

25

Despite Vincent's apprehensions, the plans to go west stood. Tom and Vincent covered the two wagons with canvas and packed them with supplies for the ten- to twelve-day trip. They also packed many of the essentials they would need to get started in Kansas: a barrel of flour, fifty pounds of navy beans, several sides of salt pork, two sacks of potatoes, spices, herbs, a bag of sugar, fifty pounds of salt, dried raisins and apples. Eggs could be bought from farmers along the way. Orel Jane and her mother both packed trunks for the trip too. Orel Jane included her spelling and arithmetic books, as well as *McGuffy's Reader*. A few pieces of furniture were stored in the little space left in the wagon. Finally, the men tied a new plow called a "grasshopper" to one side of each wagon. They secured two barrels to the other side and filled each with water.

Each day Orel Jane and her mother sewed on the wedding dress. Tom, too, prepared for the wedding. One day he came by the schoolhouse with a new suit, fancy boots and a hat, the first he had ever purchased. Orel Jane admired it all and said that he would sure look like a gentleman.

"Sure seems like a waste of money to me," Tom said, but there was pride in his eyes as he laid everything out for Orel Jane's approval.

The Sunday came in mid-March when Reverend Davis would preach his last sermon and bid farewell to the congregation. Orel Jane dressed in her prettiest light-colored dress, and Tom put on his black suit, boots and tie.

"Why, Tom, you do look like a gentleman," Orel Jane complimented him. "Your black beard and long hair blend in with your suit so well. But there is a bald spot showing on top of your head."

"Hmm. Well, you know my age by this time. This suit feels more like a straight jacket. First time I've been dressed up since I married Nancy," he said, grinning.

They sat near the front of the church, slyly holding hands. Her father gave a disapproving look, but Tom squeezed her hand anyway. After the service members gathered around to wish them luck and voice their regrets at them leaving. There were tears in Mrs. Davis's eyes.

The next day the men hitched two yoke of oxen to each of the covered wagons in front of the Davis home and loaded them. Tom and Rhodia helped, then bid a sad farewell. It was a beautiful spring day, and Tom hoped the spring rains would hold off a little. They didn't. The first day of the journey the weather turned wet and cold. The rains turned the roads, such as they were, into quagmires, forcing the travelers to slosh through knee-deep mud. When they got stuck, which was often, all eight oxen were hitched to one wagon to pull it through. Tempers flared, and by the time they got to Gentry, Orel Jane and Tom had quarreled so many times that they discussed whether it would be wise for them to get married. Mrs. Davis shushed them, while Vincent suggested that they pray for nicer weather. The weather soon cleared, and everyone felt better. A panel of wagons joined them, headed west for the "promised lands." Most, however, were headed for less dangerous parts than White Rock Valley, such as eastern Kansas, Nebraska and sometimes Colorado.

On April 1, 1865, in his small church in Gentry, Daniel performed a simple marriage ceremony. Orel Jane and Tom exchanged vows, and Tom took her in his arms and held her, giving her a long kiss. He was thirty-nine and she was twenty-three.

Mary Davis prepared a big wedding dinner for the few guests. The rest of the day was spent resting and visiting.

"Now we must hurry," Tom urged early the next morning. "We have so much to do and so little time to do it."

He stored his new suit, tie and boots in Orel Jane's trunk and helped Daniel load their wagon. At sunup three wagons headed for Kansas. Vincent's book, *Prairie Traveler*, by Randolph Marcy, proved to be an excellent guide. It gave detailed instruction for prairie travel, although it didn't say much about preparing for the Indians who might object to their homeland being invaded.

Each night Tom and Orel Jane crawled into their blankets under the wagon and talked far into the night, making future plans. Once they just lay there and watched the moon come over the horizon.

"There are tall, straight cottonwoods in a grove nearby," Tom said, describing the valley to Orel Jean. "We'll build a big log house with a fireplace in each end, one for us and one for Daniel and Mary," he boasted.

"And a big loft for the kids," Orel Jane added.

"Oh, sure."

They crossed the Missouri River at St. Joseph. When Tom crossed the river in 1849 there was a mob of wagons waiting to cross, but this time many of them were heading for places other than the gold fields or Oregon.

Wagons jammed up near the river waiting their turn to cross on the ferry, a delay that left Tom fuming. "We won't get there in time to build a cabin and plant corn," he fretted. "Come on, drivers. Don't be so slow!"

"Slow down, Tom" Orel Jane said, laughing. "Save your energy for cutting logs."

It was a large ferry and several wagons could be loaded each trip. Wheels had to be taken off upon boarding and put back on the other side of the river, another irritating delay for Tom. He howled with pain when he dropped a wheel on his foot and cursed out loud. "Now, now!" Orel Jane cautioned. His foot and his nerves felt better as they crossed the wide Missouri. He let go with an Indian whoop that White Feather had taught him when he helped fight warring tribes in the western states.

"Now take a look at Kansas!"

FOUR

Spring, 1865

Tom, Orel Jane, Daniel and Mary stood on a low hill overlooking the Republican River and the White Rock Valley beyond. Tom had his arm around Orel Jane's waist, holding her close, drinking in the scene. Daniel and Mary showed apprehension. Orel Jane was quiet, but Tom was jubilant.

"We're home!" Tom shouted, his voice echoing off the high bluffs to the southwest.

"First time you've seemed happy since we left Keokuk," Orel Jane said, laughing.

For a long time they viewed the valley: the pine-studded hills to the southwest, the tall prairie grass stretching to the hills north, the cottonwood grove south of the creek and the White Rock Creek as it raced into the river.

It was a peaceful mid-morning with a bright, warm sun shining over their shoulders. They had just arrived after a circuitous trip to Clyde. Orel Jane's parents decided to stop there, rather than cross the river, so the rest of them had helped the Davises get settled in a small home. Mrs. Davis insisted that Emery stay with them rather than accompany his mother to Indian country; Orel Jane agreed. From there Reverend Davis would become a circuit rider for the Lord and establish churches in the new land. Daniel and Mary debated long and hard—both with themselves and Tom and Orel Jane—whether to stay behind or settle in White Rock Valley. Daniel continued to stand firm against carrying weapons.

29

"We might be killed if we won't protect ourselves," Mary said. "I just don't know. . ."

"It's not just Indians that we need to protect ourselves against. There are also outlaw gangs who take advantage of the absence of law and order," Tom warned. "These outlaws, the Younger brothers, Jesse and Frank James and others, fought for the South during the war. Now they are nothing but ruthless robbers. But it is the Indians that we have to fear the most. They will stop at nothing to prevent settlers from invading their land."

Daniel was adamant. "I just can't imagine a minister taking a gun and shooting at anyone, even an outlaw or an Indian. But we'll go with you and Orel Jane." Daniel and Mary were not alone in their hesitation to cross the Republican River, but Tom never wavered; this would be their new home. He was thankful that Orel Jane never wavered ether. If she did, she didn't show it or talk about it.

Apprehension clearly showed on Daniel's face as the foursome prepared to cross the river. He withheld any remarks he may have contemplated, but he stood firm in his decision not to carry a weapon. He was dressed in dark well-worn minister's garb that looked out of place in the surroundings. The women both wore dresses: Mary her worn blue calico, Orel Jane her black dress. A colored scarf covered her head. Tom wore his usual frontier garb: buckskin jacket, britches and a soldier's cap. He wore a brace of revolvers and held his specially made repeating rifle in his right hand, the brass bullet carriage shining in the sun. He always kept his weapons in perfect condition, cleaned and polished each day—and loaded.

The river was running high because of spring rains; other times it could be waded. White Rock Creek tumbled into the river slightly to the right of where they stood. Finally Tom broke the quiet and their reveries.

"The first order of business is to get to the other side of the river, and that means we must unload the wagons and tar the boxes to make them waterproof."

The oxen, unyoked and turned loose, wandered to the river's edge and drank slowly as though tasting the water. They meandered back to the top of the knoll to graze on the tender, protein-rich grass springing up under the dead, tall bluestems.

Tom and Daniel slid the furniture and boxes from one of the wagons. The women gathered their dresses and laid them carefully on a rubber tarp on the dew-draped grass. "I trust the men know what they're doing," Mary said.

After the boxes were well tarred and considered leak proof, Tom tried to wade across the river below the rushing water from White Rock Creek. It was too deep. He tried further down and made it across, although the water was more than waist deep. "We can make it," he decided.

It took several trips—hauling small loads each time—to get the supplies and furniture over. Each trip required coaxing to get the oxen to wade through the rough current. They would slip downstream considerably before clambering up the bank on the other side. Lastly the women rode over. Mary screamed when the box tipped slightly in the rushing water. Orel Jane sat with tight lips and said nothing.

Wagons reloaded, they drove up the south side of White Rock Creek a short distance and stopped in the shade of the cottonwoods to look over the land and decide what to do next. Old Calico, leader of the oxen, led the others out to a grassy spot where they lay down and chewed their cud contentedly, seemingly aware that the arduous trip was over. Tom pulled out his binoculars and studied the hills and the trees for some time.

"There are Indians out there somewhere. They just haven't shown up yet. After the Indian wars of the past year or two, they won't likely be friendly."

Tom suggested living in the wagons for a while until he and Daniel could get a few furrows plowed for sod corn and a garden. Orel Jane argued for shelter first. "It's the first of May and it's time to plant corn," Tom argued. "We will need something to eat this fall, you know."

"No. Shelter comes first, whatever it is," Orel Jane countered.

Daniel and Mary concurred with Orel Jane. Tom gave in.

"Then it will have to be dugouts at first," Tom insisted.

"What's a dugout?" Orel Jane asked.

"Well, it's a hole in the bank," Tom explained.

Orel Jane grimaced at the thought. "Well, so be it."

That very afternoon Tom and Daniel started digging into the bluff on the south side of the creek, below the Pawnee dirt hovels built many years before. "The structures had much in common," Mary said wryly. "Dirt and mud."

Tom dug the dirt and Daniel carried it away in a wheelbarrow. "Let's make a bank of dirt a ways out," Tom suggested. "It will keep out the water if the creek floods and serve as an embankment to fight behind if Indians should attack."

Tom dug out the door; when inside he widened the hole. When it came time for dinner at noon, Orel Jane and Mary decorated a dining room table with a colorful tablecloth and set it with good china and tableware. Orel Jane brought out the camp chairs.

"It's a beautiful day for a picnic," she said.

"And sow belly never tasted better," Tom added after Dan had offered lengthy prayers, both of thanksgiving and for future protection from Indians. Orel Jane added an additional "Amen."

Day after day they dug away at the bank. When the room was large enough for a bed and furniture, Tom said it was big enough. There was no leftover room, so the women continued to cook outside. Laundry facilities were scarce; wet clothes hung on a line between trees. And there was still no outhouse; they simply ran into the woods.

With one dugout complete, the men began work on a second. Daniel and Tom cut logs and made a frame in front of each hole over which they hung a curtain cut from the wagon canvas tops. Neither of the women was especially enthusiastic about putting their furniture and kitchen stuff in the dark, damp holes.

After the dugouts were finished, Daniel and Tom hitched two yoke of oxen to a plow and cut a furrow a quarter of a mile long almost straight south. Old Calico and Blacky led the team. Daniel guided the oxen, geeing and hawing a straight lie, while Tom held the plow handles. It was a back-breaking job; tough grass roots, untouched for hundreds of years, jarred the handles out of his hands. After each furrow Tom stopped to sharpen the plowshare. It was enough to make even a strong man curse under his breath—if not out loud—and sometimes Tom did.

One day they plowed. The next day they cut holes in the sod with an ax and dropped in kernels of corn. At the near end of the furrows Orel Jane and Mary planted potatoes, beans, lettuce and other garden crops. They took advantage of the days of sunshine and worked from daylight until dark, then dropped into bed exhausted to dream of a big crop of corn, garden stuff and a future cabin near the cottonwoods.

***

One day Tom saw a herd of buffalo go over a hill not far away to the northwest, so Daniel and he went hunting.

"We're going along," Mary and Orel Jane insisted. The four set off, with only Tom carrying a rifle. "You'll have your own gun, Orel Jane, as soon as we find a gunsmith," Tom said.

When they came near the low hill Tom crawled to the top on his hands and knees then dropped flat on his belly. The rest sat quietly on the wagon. Tom had instructed them not to make a sound that might frighten the grazing animals.

Soon they heard the powerful buffalo gun roar, followed by the rumble of the animals as they raced over the next hill. Tom motioned to Dan to bring the wagon.

"Got a fine young cow," Tom said, pointing to the animal as it breathed its last breath. He had shot her through the heart.

The men began skinning, Tom making a long swipe down the belly and up each leg. Finally they had the hide spread out and the carcass lying in the middle. Tom gutted it and cut the carcass into quarters. Last of all he cut out the tongue, "a special delicacy."

The quarters were laid on sheets in the wagon with the hide spread over them, hide down. On the way back to the creek they passed a large bed of wild roses. The women insisted on stopping to dig a few to set around the new dugouts.

At home, Tom laid the hide on the ground to be prepared for tanning. He drove stakes through the hide around the edges and stretched it. Some of the animal's innards would be worked into the hide during the first tanning step, as he had been taught by friendly Indians in the West. Each morning Tom worked the hide until it was dried and flexible.

Tom cut huge steaks from the enormous hump. Quarter-portions he hung high on an outstretched cottonwood limb so that they would be kept cool at night and not spoil for as long as possible. The rest was cut into jerky strips and hung on a line between the trees to dry.

33

After preparing the buffalo, Tom and Dan began to cut cottonwood logs for a twelve-by-thirty-foot cabin. Their plan called for the families to live in opposite ends of the cabin, both of which would include a fireplace. The stones for the fireplace would come from exposed rocks near Round Mound to the south. A ridge pole would be laid from end to end. There their plans seemed to peter out.

"I don't know much about building a cabin, Daniel. How about you?" Tom asked.

"Me either, but we can learn together."

Tom surveyed the cottonwood grove, staring at a tall, straight tree for some time. Lazy clouds hung overhead. A squirrel chattered from a limb. "We need straight ones for the base logs. Right?"

"Yeah, but let's lay stones first for them to sit on."

"Then let's hitch up and get them from Round Mound. First we'll have to split a few logs for a stone boat."

To find suitable logs for splitting, they had to go to the hills southwest, a trip which took several days. When they had finished the boat they hitched two yoke of oxen to it and used it to bring back a load of stones from Round Mound. While there, Tom climbed the mound and searched for signs of Indians. He saw none, but he had an excellent view of the country for miles south and north. Deer, elk and antelope grazed on the flats to the south. The Indians remained elusive, but one day smoke signals could be seen from a faraway hill. "They're talking about us," Tom said, smiling.

Back at their camp the men dug a trench a couple of feet wide for the foundation, then dug in the stones every few feet. Tom took a long string and stretched it above the stones, adjusting them until they were perfectly even and level.

"Now let's cut that tree we've been looking at for a ridge pole," Tom suggested. After a long look Dan said, "It'll do."

Tom's adz came into play as they vigorously squared logs for the sides and the ends of the cabin. Orel Jane and Mary came during the middle of the afternoon with steak sandwiches and hot coffee.

"What of the floor?" Orel Jane asked with a grimace, envisioning a dirt floor such as those in the dugouts.

"We'll get straight cedars from the hills and I'll split puncheon for the floor," Dan said. "Tom can prepare the rest of the logs for the walls." Tom helped Dan get the logs from the hills. They took the box from the running gears and used a long rope to roll timber up a long ramp onto the gears. Dan took his time and selected straight timber. While Dan split logs for the floor, Tom squared cottonwood logs for the walls. He notched each log so that it fit perfectly at each corner. Tom notched holes five feet high for portholes but not without an argument over them with Dan. "Won't be needed," Dan said.

"But they'll be there if we do."

Dan sawed a hole in each end for the fireplaces, which created both a problem and a challenge. Tom studied the walls for a whole day and then studied the stones at Round Mound, then proceeded with construction. At first it wasn't much of a problem to lay up the heavy stones, but as the fireplace and chimney rose higher, it became more difficult to hoist up the rocks. Dan built a scaffold and a log ramp, the sweat pouring from him as the hot sun beat down. "We ought to do this in the fall and winter," he said.

"But winter is when we'll need it," Tom countered, hoisting another rock up the ramp and placing it. Daubing muddy clay around it, he made ready for another, flipping the surplus mud off and wiping his hands on his pants. Dan mixed more clay in a tub.

Occasionally Dan would stand back and survey Tom's work and suggest he move this way or that so that the fireplace would be halfway straight.

"You sure are particular," Tom snorted one day as he neared the top. "But I guess we wouldn't want it to fall over, would we?"

"I am particular whether I'm building a cabin or preaching a sermon," Dan said, grinning.

When Tom grumbled and let fly a profane word or two the womenfolk brought more sandwiches and coffee. Finally the troublesome job was finished and a pleasant-looking fireplace stood at each end of the cabin.

Dan mixed more mud from the clay hauled from Round Mound. From this they daubed the cracks in the logs. If Dan allowed any mud to fall into the portholes, Tom carefully came along and removed it.

To prove to Dan that he intended for the portholes to stay, Tom brought out his rifle, slid it through one of the portholes and sighted a distant sapling. He pulled the trigger and cut the sapling square in two. "Good shot," Orel Jane complimented.

That brought a frown to Daniel's face. "We haven't seen one sign of Indians."

"Just wait. It's the ones you don't see that get you," Tom warned. They would never agree on how to get along with the Indians, and Tom would never get Daniel to carry a gun or learn to use one. Sometimes their disagreements led to heated arguments.

"Of course," Tom argued, "I would never deliberately shoot an Indian without being fired on, as some people do. But if I am under attack I will shoot and shoot to kill. I sympathize with their cause. But white men will take the land—of that I'm sure."

"But to kill is murder no matter what the provocation," Daniel argued.

"The Israelites killed and drove out the heathens when they settled the Holy Land," Orel—who knew her Bible about as well as Daniel—countered. "But if I were the Indians I would fight just as hard as they are to keep my homeland."

With the exception of their occasional arguments concerning the Indian problem, the two couples got along very well. Each respected the other's point of view, a necessary ingredient for living together in the loneliness of the valley. The women managed to provide food for the two families despite their primitive cooking facilities. They had to cook outdoors with kettles hung on a bar over the fire and water hauled from the clear White Rock stream. Tom's old but well-traveled Dutch oven stayed hot most of the time as Orel Jane and Mary baked bread, biscuits and corn bread. Fresh vegetables and potatoes provided the pioneers with fine meals and balanced diets, although none of them worried about such things.

When the weather was pleasant the couples enjoyed sitting and eating under the spread of the huge cottonwood nearby. But when it turned wet and cold—well, that was another matter. Then they often ate cold roast and cold biscuits. Orel Jane often baited a hook and caught fine bass, bullheads and catfish, and a few trout, all good size. "What a pleasant change of diet," Mary would exclaim.

The work on the cabin progressed, with Daniel doubling as both carpenter and preacher. They built the roof from Daniel's split logs, which were laid as close together as possible. Over this they spread a mixture of clay and chopped hay, which was soon as hard as a rock. The men hoped it would shed water and not leak too much, but Tom was not convinced; he had seen too many adobe shacks along the Overland Trail. "Usually the dried mud cracked and leaked like a sieve when a good rain came along," Tom said doubtfully.

Once the cabin had a roof, the men concentrated on indoor furnishings. Daniel split logs and built cabinets and shelves, as well as benches on which to sit. Lofts were constructed in each end, and Daniel built a ladder for each. Finally there was just one essential piece of furniture the cabin still lacked: beds. Daniel's puncheon boards were used to build one in each end of the cabin; willow limbs substituted for mattresses. Orel Jane and Mary brought in the little furniture they had: a dresser, small tables and some chairs. Mary hung a picture on one wall. "We'll get more furniture when we get to Manhattan," Tom assured Orel Jane.

Daniel had enough split timber to build a new long table down the center and more benches. He was already thinking of using the cabin for church services, although they were as yet the only settlers in the valley.

"Praise the Lord, it is finished," Daniel shouted jubilantly as he finished off the last of the benches. The couples celebrated with a big picnic dinner under the cottonwood.

***

After the cabin was finished, Tom and Daniel began to plan the barn and corral. Their conference took place one morning after breakfast over several extra cups of coffee.

"We don't want it near the creek and the trees. If a blizzard comes along it might pile over and cover the barn and corrals," Tom said. "We don't want it east of the house to interfere with seeing Indians approaching. How about putting it southeast of here, not too far from the cabin?"

All agreed to this, although Daniel refused to worry about Indians and outlaws.

Tom and Daniel went to work again. Using cottonwood logs, they built the barn about twenty-by-twenty feet square, with a big door to the south. The building was barely large enough for all the oxen. The corral was built with posts set every ten feet with a pole on top. They cut willow brush from near the creek and set this upright against the poles and anchored it with grapevines.

"Next year we'll build a good pole corral and fence a small pasture the same way," Tom asserted. "It's getting tiresome staking out the oxen and I'm afraid to let them run loose too much. I know Indians don't care for cows but they could run them off just to be a nuisance or as a joke."

Through all the construction and planning, Tom and Daniel continued to work well together. Their good relationship was based partially on necessity, but it was unusual for two men to get along so well, considering they had so little in common. Not that Tom wasn't religious—it just didn't show as much in him as it did Daniel. Tom talked a lot during the evenings, especially when he reminisced about his experiences out West. He sometimes recalled his harrowing experience in Death Valley, where he nearly died of thirst. He also told of his friendship with White Feather, a friendly Indian who for whatever reason had deserted his own people and decided to fight them along side white men in California during the Civil War. Tom studied Indian tactics and culture under White Feather. It was White Feather who taught him to aim at one Indian, then another, when under attack and they, not sure who might die first, would hold their fire.

The captain never fully trusted him, but White Feather proved his loyalty after a small tribe wiped out a new settlement, killing everyone and burning the village. He located the tribe in a mountain village and helped surround them at night. The soldiers killed the entire tribe, but in the fight White Feather was killed. They buried him with full military honors along with the fallen soldiers.

Orel Jane kept her notebook handy and recorded these stories and many others, not while Tom was talking—he clammed up when he saw her get out her notebook and pencil—but later, when he was asleep or during the daytime. Daniel was quieter, saying little except when he talked about the Lord and future plans for churches in the valley.

By the time the cabin was halfway livable it was late August—time to cut hay for the oxen and the sole milk cow. Tom sharpened the scythe with his whetstone, and he and Daniel went forth to tackle the tough waist-high grass, laying it down in neat swathes. Later they stacked it near the barn.

Every day Tom scanned the trees along the creek for signs of Indians. Occasionally a few rode into sight far up the valley, but they showed no signs of hostility. He frequently checked the distant hill with his binoculars.

During one of their many walks in the valley, Tom and Orel Jane covered some ten miles; deer, antelope and elk scampered out of their way. The young ducked behind their mothers to peek around at the strangers. Farther up the valley, nearly out of sight, they could see buffalo cows nursing their calves. A rattlesnake rattled from behind a rosebush, while a raccoon chattered from a treetop. Wild flowers bloomed in profusion. North of White Rock Creek they found a big patch of wild rosebushes and Tom dug up several more to take home to plant in their yard.

"I never dreamed this valley would be so beautiful," Orel Jane commented as they stood and drank in the sights.

***

The war between the states was over; the war with the Indians was not. The army was trying its best to get the Indians to accept reservation life and the Indians were just as determined to resist. They were making their last stand on the high plains, a region that had long been known as the Great American Desert and, by inference, fit only for Indians. For 200 years the Indians had been pushed westward by settlers claiming the East Coast. Now the West Coast was becoming settled, squeezing the Indians from the other direction. In addition, white settlers were pouring into the plains like grasshoppers on the march. The new homestead law, which allowed a person to own a quarter-section of land if he improved it and lived on it for five years, sped up the process. All treaties with the Indians would be broken to accommodate this march. Illustrious Civil War soldiers, such as Sherman, Kidder, Crook and Custer were sent west to bring order to the plains. They would be the last to say they were succeeding.

Custer, other generals, and a few of the scouts, such as Buffalo Bill and Colonel Frank North, stopped often at the Lovewell home during that winter of 1865. It was a convenient stopover in their trips between western forts and Fort Riley. They offered the Lovewells and the Davises valuable information about the various tribes and how to protect themselves in case of attack.

These Indian fighters spent hours recounting Indian troubles. The Pawnee were fairly peaceful, they explained. The Sioux tribes were the troublemakers, not only fighting the white man but also their historical enemy, the Pawnee. The Sioux, Comanche, Arapaho and other plains tribes could be cruel. Their worst trick, the one most feared by white women, was to kidnap a woman and force her to become the chief's slave and the women's chore girl.

Such actions often resulted from the Indians' anger: anger over the infringements on their homeland and the needless wrecking of their commissary—the slaughter of the buffalo herds. Many were killed for their hides because of the big demand for furs and leather, while the valuable meat was left to rot. Sympathy back East was with the Indians; General Custer and others knew they were no heroes back there.

The Indians were determined warriors who had no intentions of fighting the way the army thought they should. They struck with lightning speed and were gone as quickly. They hung onto the off-side of their mounts and shot from under their horses' necks, making them a poor target for the soldiers. The soldiers took out after them, but the Indians scattered and hid in the numerous canyons of central Kansas, where soldiers could never find them.

But the Indians laid low in winter. They put up no hay for their ponies, which fended for themselves. It took them a while in the spring to regain their strength and get some meat on their ribs, which is why settlers felt safer in winter and early spring. This custom would lead to the Indians' downfall. Custer eventually decided that if the Indians were to be conquered he would have to strike in subzero weather. Later he did just that.

Despite his conflicts with them, Custer admired the Indians. "They're called the world's best cavalry men," he said one evening during a winter stopover at the cabin. "I agree. Once we shot an Indian off his horse. Two companions rode in, reached down, picked him up and rode away. We watched and let them get away with it. But they are tricky and cruel, never forget that."

Because of the color of his hair the Indians called Custer "Yellow Hair." He was studious and often quiet, sitting before the blazing fire without saying a word for an hour at a time. The Lovewells and the Davises always waited patiently for him to resume. Orel Jane filled coffee cups again and again and later took notes.

Buffalo Bill was another frequent guest at the Lovewell-Davis cabin. His tone was boastful, and Tom thought his stories often seemed questionable. But he was fun to have around, and he was a good storyteller.

Prior to the Civil War, when Bill was young, his father had died at the hands of an outlaw pro-slavery gang, leaving Bill the man of the house at a young age. Tom found that story hard to believe.

More enjoyable was Bill's story about his twenty-mile walk behind a mule that got loose when he was riding from Fort Dodge to Fort Larned. He volunteered to take a message to Fort Larned when no one else would. The land was infested with hostiles, but the fort was special to Bill since it was his home base.

Twenty miles out he stopped for a drink of water at a stream. His ornery old mule did likewise, then walked away. Bill tried to catch him but he always managed to stay some distance ahead. Bill got madder each step he took.

Finally, towards morning, he heard the morning gun at the fort. The mule brayed in triumph at the same time, standing broadside, silhouetted against the morning sun. Bill, footsore and angry enough to skin that mule alive, raised his rifle, took aim, and boom, that mule tumbled over dead. This alarmed the garrison, which prepared for battle, but Bill's arrival explained everything.

Despite the Indian scout's warnings, it was a quiet winter at the Lovewell-Davis cabin. Nevertheless, it would soon become apparent that White Rock Valley was not immune to the red man's cruelty.

FIVE

Spring, 1866

Orel Jane took aim at the target with her new rifle and hit the bull's-eye. She tried again with the same results. "Those ol' Indians better be careful around you now," Tom complimented her.

"But I hope I never need to use it on them," she said. "I would rather shoot buffalo."

"You can do that too."

They were at the armory in Clifton. Tom had insisted that Orel Jane take rifle training sponsored by the local militiamen. The commander encouraged settlers to do this to protect themselves against Indians. Tom went uptown to trade a yoke of oxen for a span of mules and Orel Jane continued to practice.

When Tom came back he presented her with a new Spencer six-shot carbine. She rewarded him with a kiss.

"I'll be gone a lot and I want you to be able to protect yourself and the family."

Orel Jane fired at the target with the new carbine and missed the bull's-eye. Tom adjusted the sights and she emptied the chamber, hitting the target perfectly. "You can handle it," Tom congratulated her. "Now let's get back to your parents and get ready to go to Manhattan. It's a five-day trip, you know."

They were on their way to Manhattan to buy supplies and had stopped over for a few days with her parents to see Emery. Her parents were opposed to her taking rifle lessons but then they were opposed to them living in the White Rock Valley at all. It was too early; travelers brought back too many horror stories from the west. Her mother remained firm in her insistence that Emery stay with them.

They followed a segment of the Overland Trail that followed the Republican River, dodging the traffic as they headed southeast. The trail, which had been used for many years, was a popular route seventeen years before, when thousands of homesteaders made their way to Oregon and other western states. Now the wagons that clogged it carried scores of immigrants heading west to take homesteads on the plains. Mixed in were numerous freight wagons. Rail lines were under construction but wouldn't be completed for a few years yet.

Tom would pull off to the side every afternoon to find good grass and hobble the mules. At camp each evening, conversations turned to where each party was going and what they dreamed of accomplishing.

The third night, before entering Manhattan, they camped on a hill east of the trail. Tom approved of the grass, but he eyed some nearby bushes suspiciously. After inspecting them thoroughly he rejoined the others. "Don't want any surprises," he said when he came back.

Orel Jane cooked up a big batch of stew in the Dutch oven that included buffalo jerky, plus potatoes and beans from her own garden.

"We eat at a fancy restaurant tomorrow night," Tom said. That brought a smile from Orel Jane.

Manhattan was a busy city, the hub of businesses that catered especially to travelers' needs. Tom left the team with the livery man and they headed for the fanciest restaurant in town.

It was fancy all right; the waiters wore black suits, the tables were set with costly silverware. They studied the menu. "Guess what?" Tom said, "they serve buffalo steaks."

"Suits me," Orel Jane said.

Tom talked to the manager about supplying the restaurant with buffalo meat. "Sure we'll take it, but only if it's quality meat," the manager said. "Too often it's tough."

Orel Jane even talked Tom into taking her to a stage play at the nearest theater. "Our honeymoon," Tom said and held her hand. She kissed him on the cheek, right there in public.

They shopped all day and loaded the wagon. Packed in tightly were a barrel of flour, boxes of dried fruit, rolls of calico dress goods, bags of coffee, cans of herbs and a jug of whiskey. The latter for medicines and snake bites, Tom said when Orel Jane objected. The last to be loaded was a cast-iron cookstove for Orel Jane and a rocking chair for Tom. At the haberdashery he looked for work clothing.

"Have you heard about Levi Strauss' canvas pants?" asked the owner. "He started making them in California from the canvas tops of abandoned wagons. Miners needed something that was tough and would stand up to their hard, rough work. They're tough and hard to tear."

Tom bought two pairs, then stopped to talk about gold mining and living in the gold state until Orel Jane came looking for him. "You always stop to talk too much," she grumbled.

At the United States land office Tom filed on the two eighty-acre homesteads, one for them and one for the Davises. Now they could say it was official: they were the first permanent settlers in White Rock Valley—if the Indians let them stay. The office was filled with other men filing on homesteads too. Kansas would settle up quickly.

On the second night of the return trip they camped at the site with the good grass and suspicious bushes, which Tom re-inspected. He liked the spot because they could see all around; there was less chance of surprises, too.

He hobbled the mules and, after supper, he and Orel Jane slept under the wagon. Tom kept his guns handy, Orel Jane's as well as his own.

The next morning Tom went to get the mules, which had grazed quite a ways from the wagon. He came back with one mule carrying the other mule's broken hobble.

"He's nowhere in sight," Tom told Orel Jane, "but I'm sure he headed for Clifton. I'll jump on this mule and run him down. I won't be gone long, but you keep that gun handy."

Orel Jane watched nervously as Tom disappeared over the hill. She spent the day watching the north skyline. She could see wagons going up the river but they paid little attention to her. Sometimes she huddled behind those bushes a distance from the wagon. She recalled everything she had ever learned about Indians and how they attacked a wagon. She remembered that they usually captured or killed the owners. Then they attached themselves to what they liked, such as gaily colored calico, and

45

burned the wagon. She had visions of them riding off in her gingham cloth and taking her prisoner to become the chief's slave. That night she lay down with the carbine in hand, never sleeping a wink. The next morning she returned to her vigil in the bushes. If they burned the wagon she would do nothing; if they came her way she would shoot.

All day she fretted. What could have happened to Tom? Her fear increased by the hour. "Is he hurt? Has he been killed?" These horrible thoughts followed each other through her head continually. By noon she was terrified, frantically trying to decide what to do. It shouldn't have taken Tom that long to catch up with the mule and return.

At about 4:00 she heard what sounded like someone coming. She cocked her gun and hid herself again. When a rider came over the north hill she started to run until she realized it was Tom, riding one mule and leading the other. She ran to him, crying and laughing all at the same time. He jumped off and they hugged each other without saying a word.

"I thought the Indians had gotten you for sure," Orel Jane cried.

"That dang fool mule got back to Clifton," he explained. "I have been riding that dang mule since I left, and I'm so sore that I can hardly stand up."

The next morning they climbed aboard the wagon, seated themselves on boxes of groceries and drove up the congested trail, which was full of creaking wagons and drivers cursing their oxen and mules. Sounds carried long distances in the quiet morning air and they could hear children and mothers chatting and laughing. The traffic raised incredible amounts of dust on the trail—which in some places was as much as ten miles wide—making breathing difficult.

Orel Jane leaned against Tom and snoozed, catching up on her lost sleep during the previous two days. Tom clucked to the mules, sometimes cursing them under his breath, still not ready to forgive the one for the trouble he had caused.

***

"By the way, Orel Jane," Tom said. "In Clifton I learned that the first settlers in our valley were Mr. and Mrs. William Harsberger, Mr. and

Mrs. Asbury Clark and child, and John Furrows, all from Knox County, Illinois."

His story was interrupted when one of the mules took the bit in its mouth and headed for Clifton, refusing to take the turnoff home. Tom pulled on the lines and yelled but to no avail. Pulling out his new rawhide bullwhip, Tom flicked the mule along its shoulders and head. The mule shook its head and changed its mind.

"Back to my story. These folks left Illinois in early spring, determined to homestead in this valley that they had heard so much about. It was two years before the Indian Wars of 1864, and the Indians were still friendly. They picked sites about where we settled on White Rock Creek, built cabins and sheds, and plowed the sod for corn.

"One day Mrs. Clark went to visit her sister, Mrs. Harsberger, leaving her five-year-old son with his father. Soon after she left a band of 'noble red men,' arrayed in all the paraphernalia of savage life, made an appearance. Clark left abruptly, (hoping to find help). A little later a settler from down the creek came by the cabin to find the son showing his visitors everything the cabin contained. They were much amused and amazed by it all. Clark came back about the time the visitors left, but the storyteller says he didn't invite them back.

"In mid-summer the Pawnee returned to hunt in the valley. This was their favorite hunting ground and they hated to give it up. While they were there a large band of Sioux rode over the hills and attacked the Pawnee. The battle raged back and forth, but the Pawnee were badly outnumbered. Finally they fled over the hill south and escaped the Sioux.

"All but one, that is. He sneaked through the brush along the creek, came to Clark's home and begged to be hidden. But Clark said he could never do that, for the Sioux would find him anyway and kill them all. You see, the Pawnee, before being killed off by smallpox, were the dominant tribe of the plains and the terror of the Sioux, Cheyenne, Arapaho and others. Once they were said to have numbered 1,400, but their numbers had decreased, and the other tribes attacked them every time they had a chance. The Sioux warriors came in the cabin and grabbed the Pawnee brave. They were going to kill him right there but Clark begged them to take him away. Honoring his request, the Sioux took him a short distance away before killing him.

47

"The Clarks were in shock. The Sioux chief suggested that the settlers leave the valley, warning that there were bloodier battles to come. The settlers left soon after and never returned."

Tom had barely finished his story when he and Orel Jane reached the Republican River. They crossed the river and drove up to their cabin, where four wagons were gathered. Daniel and Mary were visiting with several people who stood around a campfire where dinner was cooking. Tom and Orel Jane got down and shook hands all around with the folks, who explained that they were new settlers.

They introduced themselves as William Belknap; Mr. and Mrs. John Rice and children; Mr. and Mrs. Nicholas Ward and son; Al Dart; Archie Bump; Erastus Bartlett and Mr. and Mrs. John Marling and son. Orel Jane jotted their names down in her ever-handy notebook.

The next morning Tom took the men up the valley, helping them pick out choice land, showing them where to find the best timber for a house and instructing them on how to protect themselves from Indian attacks. "Always work together and always have one man act as a lookout," Tom warned.

"We haven't seen any Indians," Dart said.

"That's when you need to be most careful. It's not the ones you see that get you; it's those you don't see. They're experts in sneak attack and seem to come out of nowhere."

Tom worked with the men all day, helping them mark off quarter-sections of the best land. Most of them took land on the south side of White Rock Creek, but the Wards took a homestead on the north side. They built as close to the creek as possible in order to have an available water supply and to be near each other for protection.

"If you're attacked, fire off a rifle and try to get word to us. If you can, run to the fort, which is our cabin. We'll help all we can," Tom told them before returning home. The next day Tom and Daniel pitched in and helped the settlers begin building homes.

***

When the new neighbors were settled, the Lovewells and the Davises began making plans for the homesteads they had filed on. Both

48

agreed that with the valley quickly filling up, they would be wise to increase their acreage from eighty to 160 acres each. It was agreed that the Davises would take the big cabin and the Lovewells would homestead 160 acres four miles west, where Tom had visions of establishing the town of White Rock City. The new neighbors helped Orel Jane and Tom build a smaller cabin with a fireplace on the south end and a window on each side that would allow Orel Jane to watch for Indians from any direction. They didn't forget the portholes either.

"Let's see," Orel Jane said as she viewed her new home. "We'll put the stove in the north end, the table and chairs in the middle and your rocking chair in front of the fireplace, Tom."

Tom's thoughts wandered to the tall grass outside. He would have to build sturdy, large corrals for the cattle he planned to raise on this prairie. For now, though, he and the settlers plowed and planted corn and gardens.

Come haying time it looked as if the Indian dangers had been exaggerated, and the new settlers became careless. Tom warned them to stay vigilant.

John Marling was as careful as he thought he could be, as careful as Tom said he should be. Every morning he scanned up and down the valley looking for Indians. During the day he would check again, studying the hills. He kept his rifle across the handles of his plow. He kept his horses tethered to a nearby tree when he wasn't farming in case he saw Indians coming and needed to take a fast ride to the Lovewell cabin for help.

One morning he thought he saw a party of Indians in the distance riding toward them. "I'll be right back with help. Grab your gun," he shouted to his wife, Elisabeth, as he galloped off.

John Rice and Archie Bump were having coffee with Tom and Orel Jane, discussing a possible buffalo hunt when Marling rode up and slid off his horse in front of the door.

"Indians!" he blurted.

Tom, Rice and Bump quickly mounted Tom's mules and rode up the creek, while Marling tried to describe the Indians. "I hoped they were so far away I could get help and be back before they got here."

"I just hope we're in time," Tom said as he let his mule swing into a gallop.

When they reached the cabin it was on fire, all provisions and clothing gone. The Indians had torn open the tick and feathers were flying all around.

By this time other settlers had joined the party.

"Let's go after them and rescue Elisabeth," Tom said.

"There were about forty of them," Marling said.

"We have to try."

As they rode up the valley, Tom got off and checked the tracks frequently. "Your wife and son are being led on foot," Tom said.

As they approached a grove of trees, there were signs of a struggle—including a torn piece of dress—on the ground and in the brush. Tom studied these items and scanned the area. He looked up to see Elisabeth Marling wandering about in a daze with a rope around her neck, holding her son by the hand. When she saw them she darted behind a tree, dragging the child with her. Apparently the Indians let go of Mrs. Marling and her son when they saw the settlers coming. When the men called to her and tried to approach her she ran and hid again. Calling her name again and again, Marling tried to approach her with little success. Finally she stopped to listen. When she recognized her name, she ran and threw her arms around him.

She was in shock and screaming. "I thought you were those terrible savages after me again."

Their son came running and fell into his mother's arms. Their clothes were in tatters, torn by the brush and the Indians' rough treatment.

Finally she calmed down enough to tell what happened. "They came in the cabin, grabbed my gun, and put a rope around my neck. They tried to assault me but I fought like a tiger. Then they ransacked the cabin, broke open the feather tick and set fire to the cabin. They were leading me into these trees when they saw you coming and dashed away. Oh, thank God! But we have to leave this place. I won't live in such country."

The cabin, built of green logs, was burning slowly, so the men carried water from the creek and extinguished it. They held a meeting and decided to go to Clyde.

Orel Jane's parents welcomed her and Tom and the Davises home once more. As usual, Orel's mother urged them to leave White Rock, especially upon learning Orel Jane was expecting.

"We're just thankful you are still alive. We heard all of you were killed. We hear of other massacres all over the plains."

Most of the stories proved to be untrue. After a week of loafing, Tom, Orel Jane and the Davises decided to return to White Rock Valley. "The Indians who attacked were probably renegade Sioux," Tom said.

"We'll all stay at the big cabin. We'll be safe there," Tom assured Mrs. Davis. "We won't separate until it is safe."

When they got back they found that the Wards had come back earlier. Mr. Ward had a load of buffalo meat and was taking it to Clyde to sell, which gave Tom an idea. "Let's take a load of meat to Junction City. I'll go find a good herd," he said to Orel Jane.

"I'll go with you," Orel Jane, who was not looking forward to being left alone, replied.

"Good, you can take your new carbine."

The wind was from the south so they headed for the southern hills. Buffalo have poor eyesight but they possess a good sense of smell, so it was necessary to approach a herd from the leeward side, in this case from the north. As they moved along, Tom would park the wagon, crawl to the next ridge, and look for buffalo as well as signs of Indians. Finally he came back with a report of a small herd in the next valley.

They left the wagon and crawled to the top of the ridge, creeping as close as they could without alerting the herd. It wasn't easy for Orel Jane, who was hindered both by her pregnancy and her long skirts that repeatedly became caught up in the tall grass. When they were as near as they could get, Tom showed her how to lie flat and prop the gun on her forearm and elbow.

"Lie flat?" she objected. "Well, hardly. I'll do the best I can."

He had her pick out a young bull. She took careful aim and fired; the bull dropped without moving. "Not bad!" Tom congratulated.

Both of them fired, picking young cows or young bulls. The confused herd shoved the calves into the center while the mothers faced the enemy, whatever it was. When they had enough for a load they ran forward to cut the throats of the dead animals and skin them out. The herd dashed away.

51

At home the carcasses were hung on cottonwood limbs to cool and the hides stretched out to dry before tanning. Tom began preparing his sugar-cure brine which consisted of:

> five gallons of water
> seven and one-half pounds of common salt
> one and one-half pounds of sugar, and,
> one pound, six ounces of Prague powder

The brine was tested by dropping in a potato; when it floated halfway up it was just right.

Tom brought six wooden barrels from Clyde when they returned. Orel Jane had vetoed living in their new home after the Indian troubles, so Tom stored the barrels in their unused cabin, where he also cured the meat.

Tom began by preparing five gallons of brine for each barrel. He then cut the meat into chunks and dropped them into the brine, which splashed onto his new pants, turning them a dirty whitish gray. He wiped it off but it didn't help much. The brine burned his hands and earned him a scolding from Orel Jane, who would gripe about trying to wash it from his shirt. After adding the meat chunks, Tom covered the barrel with cheesecloth to keep out insects and dirt. In thirty days he declared it cured. He cut off a roast and gave it to Orel Jane to cook in the fireplace. The aroma filled the cabin while Tom waited with anticipation and some trepidation. "What if it isn't fit to eat?" he thought.

Finally Orel Jane set the roast on a platter in the center of the table. Tom could hardly wait to carve a huge slice.

"It's just great," Orel Jane complimented after taking a bite. "We should have no trouble selling this meat." Tom smacked his lips in agreement.

"It is an especially tasty cure," Tom boasted, "one sure to please the most choosy of restaurateurs."

To double-check the meat's quality, Tom sliced off steaks for supper one afternoon. "It's just delicious," Orel Jane said as she smiled and took a mouthful from a Dutch oven-fried steak.

"Then we take a load to Junction City tomorrow."

But in Junction City Tom found little demand for buffalo meat and no restaurant would buy his. "It's tough," said one owner.

Tom was puzzled. That night they went to eat at a fancy restaurant which still served buffalo if "anyone wanted it." And Tom wasn't long in figuring out why there was no demand. The meat was tough, very tough. The reason? It was old bull beef, the very worst there was.

Tom asked for the manager. He came and Tom invited him to share a cup of coffee from their pot. "I have some very good buffalo meat for sale."

"Never. It's tough and customers won't eat it. We have to throw it out."

"Yes, but I think you bought bull meat, which is tough and has a bad taste," Tom answered. "I kill young cows and young bulls. My meat is sugar-cured and you'll like it. I guarantee it."

The manager still said no.

"Sir, I'll make you a deal. I'll furnish the meat for supper free. If your customers like it, you pay me $100 for the rest of the load."

"That sounds like a good deal, but you better be right."

Tom and Orel Jane ate there the next night. They watched with satisfaction as customers praised the dinner and even asked for seconds. The delighted owner quickly paid for the load. "Bring another load as soon as possible," he added.

Tom and Orel Jane went home planning to butcher more buffalo and take the meat to Junction City. From then on selling was no problem. Tom's sugar-cured buffalo hams were especially popular, although he also sold fresh meat during the winter.

On December 25, 1866, the Wards, the Rices and Bartlett gathered at the Davis-Lovewell cabin for their first Christmas in the valley. Orel Jane and Mary served a big Christmas dinner of fresh buffalo meat and all the trimmings. Other goodies from their garden, including potatoes, beans, carrots and beets came from the dugouts—which were now root cellars—that had served as their first homes. The men and guests praised the dinner highly.

Daniel read the story of the first Christmas from the Bible, made a few remarks and closed with a prayer of thanksgiving for a bountiful harvest and safety from the Indians.

There were a few gifts for the children, mostly homemade. Late that afternoon they were still visiting when Orel Jane said, "My time has

53

come." Mrs. Ward took over as midwife, and that evening little Josephine came into the world. As far as they knew she was the first white child born in White Rock Valley.

Long after midnight when the guests finally left, Tom watched as Orel Jane nursed the child. Then he took his daughter in his arms and held Orel Jane's hand. "She'll be the first of many," he said, grinning. Orel Jane smiled back and Josephine went to sleep in his arms. Tom lay her close to his wife, kissed her and sat down beside her while he continued to hold Orel Jane's hand.

Again that winter, frontiersmen, scouts and army personnel stopped often at the Lovewell cabin; it was such a handy place to stop before going on to Fort Riley, and everyone enjoyed Tom's hospitality and Orel Jane's cooking. The visitors exchanged stories about the frontier and Tom recounted his experiences in the far west. Sometimes the large cabin became overcrowded. Guests could be heard talking far into the night in the lofts, which were intended for future children. Orel Jane kept her notebook—which was nearly full—handy to jot down their reminiscences.

***

Sometimes visitors' stories were scary; others were intriguing. One of the fascinating stories travelers told was how the Pawnee obtained their first horses. During the 1500s, Coronado and his men camped on the Smokey Hill River during their first expedition into what is now Kansas. The Pawnee, then the dominant tribe on the plains, sent 200 warriors down to visit them. This was the first time the Indians had seen the strange animals these men rode that "could fly faster than an antelope." When the Spaniards returned to Mexico the warriors followed them on foot. Months later, they came back riding horses. Other tribes soon had horses that were stolen from the Spaniards or other tribes.

The Indians had little use for money; horses became their medium of exchange. A warrior's wealth was based on the number of horses he owned. Stealing horses from other tribes and from the white man became an accepted practice that was never considered morally wrong. Their zeal for obtaining horses contributed to some of the trouble in White Rock Valley.

54

The Pawnee, largely because of their horses, became the dominant tribe, and other tribes feared them. Their native homes had always been near the White Rock Valley or further south in Kansas Territory. When trappers started coming through the territory, they brought smallpox germs—some say intentionally—which the tribe contracted. They had no natural resistance and died in great numbers. They became so few in number, especially the men, that they could no longer fight off their enemies. They accepted the government's offer to settle in Nebraska Territory along the Loup River, but the White Rock Valley remained their favorite hunting ground, and they returned annually for buffalo.

Tom feared their friendliness would fade as white men continued to needlessly slaughter the Indians' food supply. "We will never kill except for meat," he promised Orel Jane.

SIX

Spring, 1867

The day the frost left the ground Tom and Dan hooked up two yoke of oxen and added to the strip they plowed the year before. It was the same cursed, back-breaking job as it was the year before. Tom tried to control his language but an expletive often escaped his lips as the plow handles were jerked from his hands.

Orel Jane and Mary again planted seeds in the garden near the house. Mary cut potatoes into quarters, being sure to leave an eye in each piece, while Orel Jane planted them in the mellow, wet soil. They followed with cabbage, carrots, beets, lettuce and tomatoes. Each night they flopped into bed to sleep the sleep of the tired and righteous and dream of another wonderful day.

It was a busy time, the second year of settlement in the White Rock Valley. New settlers, many recent arrivals homesteading new land, built temporary homes, plowed sod, and readied the ground for planting corn. The snow had melted, rains came on time and were plentiful. April was early for some crops, for there still could come a frost, but the weather was nice and warm. Josephine, resting in a basket in the shade of a tree, cooed and watched the birds above as they built nests and sang to their hearts' content. A wren warbled one way, turned and warbled the other way, warning all other birds that this was his territory and to stay out. It sounded like music to the child but it was just business as usual to the wren, which proceeded to gather sticks for her nest in a small tree.

Up the valley a couple of miles Mrs. Sutzer, a new settler and a widow, was busy around her new cabin near the creek. She planted a garden not far from a grove of trees on the south side of the creek while her boarder, Erastus Barlett, was in the grove cutting and splitting logs for his own cabin. The ring of his ax echoed in the still morning air. While Mrs. Sutzer's son played in the yard she went into the cabin and put a buffalo roast in the oven, a roast given to her by Orel Jane.

Across from Mrs. Sutzer, Nicholas and Mary Ward did the same things as the Lovewells, the Davises and Mrs. Sutzer; they plowed for corn and planted a garden. The Wards planned to visit the Lovewells in the evening. Mary and Orel Jane had become bosom friends and never failed to get together whenever they had a chance. Mary was a beautiful young woman, about twenty-three, with long, black hair. She liked colorful dresses. After her first husband died before coming West she married Nicholas Ward, who was slightly older. She married young the first time and her son, Nick, was about seven. Nicholas and Tom often hunted together, bringing back buffalo, antelope and elk. They shared generously with neighbors like Mrs. Sutzer who could then have roast buffalo for dinner.

Most of the settlers who had left after the Indian trouble the year before had returned to prepare their fields for crops. Again, they became careless. They stopped posting watchmen on the surrounding hills and stopped working together. Tom warned them but his warning went unheeded. Why worry about Indians? Their ponies wouldn't have fattened yet and they would still be in their wigwams, the settlers reasoned. New homesteaders added to the number of careless people.

On the night of April 18, two men stopped at the Lovewell home and stayed overnight, giving their names as Lappier and Vanepps. "We would like to take land farther up the creek where there is good timber," Lappier said after eating Orel Jane's big breakfast of steak and biscuits with gravy, plus black coffee, of course. "We'll take one of our wagons today and scout around."

"Want I should go along?" Tom asked. "It's about time for the Indians to be out. If they are, it could be dangerous."

"No, you're busy. We'll get along all right. Thanks just the same," Vanepps answered. "If we see the least sign of them we'll hightail it back."

They unloaded one of their wagons and left in the other, and Tom went back to his plowing. Al Dart and John Fisher came by on their way to Clifton for supplies. Al stopped to say he was headed for Junction City to file on his claim and bring back a cookstove. Their absence left the valley short of men; there weren't many even when all the men were home.

Tom came in for dinner at noon. When he had finished eating he sat down in his rocking chair for a little rest before returning to the field. Orel Jane was looking out the window to the west when she saw a team and wagon racing toward them.

"Tom, something is wrong. There's a wagon and team coming this way at high speed. I think it's those men who left this morning to find land."

Tom jumped up, grabbed his rifle off the deer antlers over the door, and ran outside. "Indians, Indians!" the men yelled as they came bouncing over the rough trail. Orel Jane instinctively reached for her rifle standing near the fireplace.

"Indians have killed two families," Lappier shouted when they stopped. "We have this wounded boy with us."

"Why that's the Ward boy," Orel Jane cried as she took him in her arms, carried him into the cabin and lay him on a buffalo robe beside Josephine. Tom plied the boy and the men with questions while Orel Jane treated his wound with laudanum, a tincture of opium. Both men and Nick Ward shared this story:

The Indians—Tom thought they were Cheyenne—came to Mrs. Sutzer's cabin on the south side of White Rock Creek first. She was preparing dinner and didn't see the three walk in. When she saw them she quickly whispered to her son to run over and warn the Wards.

The Indians sat down in the corner and demanded food, then ate all that she had prepared for her and Bartlett. When they had eaten they rose and went outdoors, just as Bartlett came around the corner of the cabin. They killed him with a tomahawk, which sent Mrs. Sutzer into a panic. She ran from the house, screaming; the Indians killed her the same way.

The Indians crossed the creek and entered the Ward cabin just after Nicholas came in for dinner. Mary was preparing dinner and, again, they demanded food. Nicholas helped her, at the same time keeping a wary eye

58

on the red men. The Sutzer boy had warned the Wards about the Indians before they got there, but Nicholas had no reason to believe they would do more than eat the whole dinner and go on. Nick Ward and the Sultzer boy sat on the bed in the corner, holding hands in fright.

Nicholas, helping his wife with dinner, was holding a platter of meat, readying to place it on the table. One of the Indians took the rifle from its hooks over the door and asked: "Will it kill a buffalo?"

"Reckon it would," Nicholas answered, without looking around. The Indian pointed the rifle at Nicholas's back, fingered the trigger for a moment, then pulled it, hitting him. He fell to the floor, blood gushing from the massive wound.

The two boys bolted out the door, with the Indians in pursuit. The boys planned to jump in the creek and hide as they had been taught but the Indians shot them as they ran. The Sutzer boy was shot through the heart and Nick Ward through the neck. Nick fell as if dead and the Indians rode back to the cabin. Mary Ward slammed the door shut and bolted it. The Indians smashed the door open with tomahawks and took her prisoner. They tied her hands behind her and shoved her onto a horse in front of a rider. The men assumed that the Indians took her south.

Sometime during the next night Nick Ward came to and staggered back to the cabin. He found the door open and stumbled over his stepfather's body. He gathered up a blanket from one of the beds, went back to the creek bank and spent the night in terror.

"We found the lad staggering around in a daze," Lappier said. "Apparently the Indians thought he was dead. We didn't see anything of Mrs. Ward. We put the lad in the wagon and rushed to your cabin."

Tom and Orel Jane got in the wagon with Lappier, leaving Vanepps with the children with instruction to keep his gun ready, and hurried back to the massacre. They searched for Mary Ward around the cabin without success. They also scouted the woods to the south, but there was no sign of her or her captors. "Kidnapped," Orel Jane cried.

Nicholas, Mrs. Sutzer and Bartlett were scalped. They gathered the bodies into the wagon and drove back to the Lovewell home, warning settlers as they went, urging them to stay at the Davis-Lovewell cabin. "You can help us bury these people, too," Tom said.

They would need four caskets but they had no lumber.

"Bartlett had a lot of split lumber," Dan suggested. "It could never be put to better use. Let's go get it."

Dan, the carpenter, with the help of the other men, carefully constructed the caskets, making a smaller one for the Sutzer boy. There was not enough lumber for all so Dan tore up part of their cabin. The blanket-wrapped bodies were carefully and lovingly laid in the caskets and placed in two wagons. Slowly they were driven to the new cemetery on the hill south of the cabin.

Daniel officiated at the funeral. There, on a knoll south of the Davis-Lovewell home, four new graves were dug. Daniel read a portion of the Scriptures, then gave a short prayer that included a request for protection for the community and the safe return of Mary Ward, and a word for the Indians who committed the murders. "He didn't need to include the Indians," Lappier muttered to Tom.

It was a quiet, subdued group that returned to the Lovewell cabin that night. It was a sad day in the valley.

The next morning the two newcomers loaded their wagons to leave. "We will never live in such barbaric country," Lappier said.

"We're going with you," Davis said.

"Us too," Orel Jane chimed in.

Tom reluctantly agreed. He didn't have the ground ready to plant corn, and who would look after the cattle across the creek? Orel Jane found a large piece of paper and wrote a note to Dart and Fisher, which she tacked on the door, telling them why they had gone and warning them about the Indians.

The creek and the river were running bank-full from spring rains. The men tarred a wagon box, hitched a team of mules to it and swam them and the wagon across the stream. Tom had built a boat to carry corn to the cattle across the creek to tide them over until the new grass came on. They loaded their possessions in the boat and hauled them across the creek to be loaded onto the wagon.

Once again, the Lovewells were back with Orel Jane's parents. And once again, Mrs. Davis tried to talk them into giving up on the valley. Tom and Orel Jane listened politely. "Just a band of outlaw Cheyennes that got a little far east," Tom said.

In a couple of weeks Tom was anxious to get back to the valley, and Orel Jane was worried about her garden. They hitched up and drove back early one morning. The corn ground was weedy and it was time to plant; Orel Jane's garden was also succumbing to weeds. Tom jumped on one of the mules bareback and rode to see about his cattle, which had grazed too far north. He wasn't worried about Indians stealing them since they didn't think much of beef, but there were outlaw white men who would steal cattle.

They found most of the settlers had returned and were busy plowing sod and planting corn. Some were building new cabins to replace those ransacked and burned by the Indian marauders. Daniel and Mary Davis returned a couple of days later.

Tom and the settlers planted corn with rifles handy; Tom even kept his brace of .45 caliber revolvers strapped on. While in Clyde, Tom bought a sharp-ended hand planter, which he used to jab holes into the ground. When he released the handles, two to three kernels dropped into the moist earth. Each night the settlers returned to the Davis cabin. Young Nick Ward, recovering from his wounds, helped Tom with the work. The first planted corn was soon popping through the ground, and Orel Jane' potatoes plants were showing.

One evening three young men with a fine team of horses hitched to a brightly painted wagon crossed the creek and pulled up in front of the Lovewell cabin.

"Put your horses in the corral, feed them and come in for supper," Tom said, "Looking for land?"

"Naw, we're goin' buffalo hunting tomorrow," one said.

"Better not," Tom warned. "Indians are on the warpath and have killed two families up the valley."

"We're not afraid. We got new Winchesters and plenty of ammunition. We can handle 'em."

"Those might be your last words. Wish I could talk you out of it."

The men ate with the Lovewells that evening and visited for a while, trying to learn what they could about buffalo hunting from Tom and Orel Jane. Tom gave them a lot of instructions for hunting big game and for fighting Indians, should they be attacked. At the same time, Tom continued to try to talk them out of going. "Come back when it's safe and

I'll take you out. Don't go out there now," he urged, as the men set up their tent and prepared for bed.

The next morning the young men were up early. After eating breakfast with the Lovewells, they were raring to get started. They sat on their wagon, ready to go. "It's a mistake," Tom cautioned for the last time. "But, if you must, be very careful. Don't both leave the wagon ever. One of you crawl to the top of the next hill and look around. Better yet, stay here awhile. Go up the valley and bring back a deer or an antelope, or an elk. They're good eating too. When it is safe I'll take you hunting myself."

"If we see the slightest sign of Indians, we'll hurry back. We'll be extra careful."

"That is the last we'll ever see of them," Orel Jane prophesied, a tear in her eyes. "And we don't even know who to notify."

Tom and Orel Jane watched them disappear past Round Mound. When they didn't return in a couple of days, Tom said it was time to look for them. He and Daniel hooked the mules to a wagon and started out in the general direction the boys said they were headed, south and west. They picked up Dart, Fisher and Flint along the way, all of whom rode mules. It was rough, unsettled country, full of deep draws and covered with tall grass. They proceeded with extra caution, checking the hills and trees with binoculars often as they rode out in ever-widening circles. Soon they found wagon tracks.

The first indication of trouble they found was a wagon coupling pin. "Typical Indian trick," Tom said. "They pull the pin while the men are away hunting, then when the men return, the Indians show up. Seeing Indians coming, they jump in the wagon to make a run for it. With the coupling pin for the doubletree gone the team runs away, leaving them stranded. We'll find the bodies not far away."

Over a knoll in a ravine they found the bodies. The obvious had occurred just as Tom had said: They were downed with spears in their backs. The Indians took the rifles and ammunition and added two fine horses to their string.

The king pin installed, the men tied the wagon to theirs, loaded the bodies and took them home for burial. An Indian peeked over a hill once but he made no effort to attack; he probably hoped he would be chased into territory where his cronies could ambush his pursuer. When the men reached the cabin, Orel Jane searched through papers in the wagon for addresses. When she found one, she wrote to the men's families in Iowa.

***

Despite the Indian scares, settlers poured into the valley, building cabins and plowing sod. It even began to look safe to Orel Jane's father and mother, who came to the cabin and stayed a few days. The cabin had plenty of room for guests; it was also large enough for church services, which were frequently held on the Davises end. Daniel split logs and propped them up on other logs for seats. He also built a podium of rough lumber, over which he hung a tanned buckskin. Tom tanned buffalo robes to cover Daniel's rough puncheon floor, and Daniel split more lumber to replace that used for the settlers caskets. The extra touches made the cabin look quite churchlike every Sunday morning.

Tom and Orel Jane would get all dressed up, put a pretty dress on Josephine, and come over from their end of the cabin to attend the service each Sunday. They sat on the front row, singing from the hymn books Vincent brought. Many new settlers attended. Tom, so tired from the week's work, often nodded off until Orel Jane poked him awake. When Josephine cried, Tom took her out into the fresh air, which often sent her to sleep.

In nice summer weather, when the services ended, all gathered under the spreading cottonwood tree for dinner. Everyone contributed what they had, which was mainly supplied by their gardens, and there was always buffalo roast cooked by Orel Jane.

"If you think it is safe, we might move here," Orel Jane's father, Vincent, said after the services one Sunday. "This is such a beautiful valley. These people need a shepherd and so do many out beyond."

"We haven't had Indian troubles of late. Maybe it's safe," Tom answered.

One morning soon after that Vincent and Andrew Bump came through looking for land. Vincent was really thinking of settling in the valley. Bump, who settled earlier but left after the first Indian tragedy, was ready to return.

"The valley is ready for a real church," Vincent said. "Pretty soon there'll be a town that will need a place of worship. Andrew and I are going up the valley to find a good homesite, then we will all move here."

After another round of the ever-present black coffee, the two men drove up the valley. Orel Jane went back to her gardening, while Tom went out to tend his crops.

Less than three hours later Orel Jane looked up from her gardening to see the ox cart coming slowing, her father slumped over in the seat. She dropped her hoe and came running.

"We've been shot," he said weakly, slumping over the side of the cart into Orel Jane's arms. Tom came running to help lift him from the cart and carry him in the house. He bled badly. Bump lay dead in the wagon box.

Vincent was laid on a buffalo hide and Orel Jane hustled around to find muslin cloths with which to dress his wound. While they treated him as best they could, he, in a voice so low they could scarcely understand, told what occurred. "We saw these men with a peddler wagon a ways off but thought nothing about it, thinking they were looking for land too," Vincent told them. "Then we heard shots. Bump died instantly with a bullet in his heart. I was shot in the back. I tried to hang on, letting the oxen pick their way home."

Tom formed a posse at once, which went up the valley looking for the men. They followed their trail into the hills. Every now and then they found a skillet or pan dropped from the wagon. "Not hard to follow, are they? They're moving, hoping to escape us," Tom said. "But they can't outrun us."

Over a hill and in a deep draw, they came upon the wagon. It was brightly painted red and green and covered with tarpaulin over stays. Pans and pots hung on each side. The two jumped from the wagon and peered around the other side, rifles aimed at the posse.

"Better give up," Tom shouted. The two held a quick consultation, then dropped their guns and came forward. "We think you killed a man and we want to know why. The other man you shot is my father-in-law."

"We didn't kill nobody," one of the men said.

"We'll decide that when we get you to our cabin. Drop your guns and drive back."

The two proclaimed their innocence all the way back. "We're peddlers. We thought they were competing with us," one said.

"That is no excuse for killing," Tom countered.

Vigilante court was held at the Lovewell-Davis cabin. After a short conference, the posse voted to hang the peddlers. Two wagon tongues were placed in an "A" shape, and a rope was hung with a hangman's loop. All the while the men proclaimed their innocence. The first man was commanded to mount a mule. A rope was placed around his neck, and a hangman's knot was tied. Someone slapped the mule on its rump, causing it to jump and leave the man hanging. The process was repeated on the second man. When the gory deed was finished, both men were buried near Round Mound. "Don't need them in our cemetery," Tom said.

Orel Jane and Tom took her father to Clifton and found a doctor.

"I can't hold out much hope. He has lost so much blood and his lungs are severely injured," the doctor said after his examination. (Vincent never recovered from his wounds and died two years later of lung fever.)

***

Orel Jane and Tom sat around the breakfast table discussing a buffalo hunt to ensure a winter meat supply. Fall was the best time for the hunt, because the buffalo would be fat, their meat prime and tender. Just then Orel Jane looked out to see a young man walking toward the cabin. He was almost naked, with only a breach clout (piece of cloth) for a covering. "Why, it's an Indian," she said.

"He's no Indian," Tom said. "He's tanned all right but too pale for an Indian. He doesn't have Indian features, either."

When he came nearer he called out the familiar Indian greeting. Tom and Orel Jane took him in and gave him breakfast. He talked a lot, both in English and the Sioux language. It was hard to get him to talk about his past, where he was from and so forth. They guessed his parents had been killed and that he had been captured by the Indians and lived among them for a time. As he talked it became plain he was not quite "right." "Perhaps his experiences have affected his mind," Orel Jane said.

"He probably became insane and the Indians kicked him out. They're superstitious about crazy people. But what can we do with him? We can't send him on," Tom said.

"Give him some of your clothes and he can sleep in the loft," Orel Jane suggested.

He gave his name as Jim Jones, but Tom called him Crazy Jim because his actions were so unpredictable. Sometimes he ran and yelled just like an Indian youth, exhibiting some of the disgusting habits he had picked up from the Indians—habits that no one talked about in mixed company. It worried Orel Jane to have him around little Josephine.

Jim was always unpredictable. He would run away from the house and let go with a perfect imitation of an Indian war cry that would bring Orel Jane running from the cabin, gun in hand. Neighbors would come racing to the cabin, thinking they were under attack. Once he made a bow and arrow of straight willow limbs and began firing away at birds and rabbits, and he sometimes brought in small game for Orel Jane to cook. When he was upset or angry he spoke in Sioux, which frustrated and angered Orel Jane as much as anything. It bothered Tom when he slipped up on him with perfect stealth, totally unnoticed until he spoke. Instinctively, Tom nearly fired on the lad once. "We have to get rid of him one way or another before I kill him," he fumed to Orel Jane.

The restaurant in Junction City needed more buffalo meat, so Tom and Daniel decided to go hunting. Orel Jane asked them to take Crazy Jim with them. They found a small herd in the northern hills and were preparing to shoot when Crazy Jim ran out and tried to catch a buffalo calf. This spooked the herd, which ran up the draw and out of sight over a hill. Tom was so furious—all he could do was stand and curse the lad. "Might as well go home. Can't hunt with him along," Tom fumed.

Back home, Tom told Orel Jane the lad must go. "Maybe we can get him to some relative back East."

A few days later hide hunters came along with a load of buffalo hides. They consented to take the boy with them.

***

The next day the neighbors got together to plan a major buffalo hunt for their winter meat supply. They would also kill extra buffalo for the market. The money they earned was a good source of income for those low on money, which included about everybody.

"We may have to go quite a ways, so we may be gone overnight. Keep your gun handy," Tom cautioned Orel Jane.

Two days later they were back with wagons loaded with choice meat. Tom immediately began to prepare meat for their winter supply and for the restaurant in Junction City, which wanted more of his sugar-cured hams. He kept the less desirable cuts for personal use and made a lot of jerky. For something to chew on when someone was away from home for any reason, jerky couldn't be beat—especially on that long trip to Junction City.

The Lovewells, like the rest of the settlers, had to be content with make-shift conveniences, including those made from the plentiful buffalo hides. Tom had saved one large buffalo hide and tanned it. Half of it he folded and used to cover a lounge he made of poles. He used a portion of the other half for a mattress and part of it he hung over the cabin entrance for a door. The rest, which had a large bullet hole in it, he draped over a chair he kept in the yard. There he could sit and rest during the evening and watch the sun go down.

That evening, after the men returned, Orel Jane told Tom of her scare while he was gone. "You remember that leftover hide you draped over that chair out there? Well, my tame ducks were making a lot of noise so I went out to see what was bothering them, rifle in hand. I thought maybe coyotes or wolves might be after them. I saw what I thought was an animal eye, so I carefully took aim and fired. When I heard a dull thud I realized I hit the hole in that hide. Anyway, after that the ducks settled down, so whatever was bothering them went away."

Tom kidded her about shooting up his chair but complimented her on her marksmanship. "Thankfully it was nothing more than an animal bothering you."

In order to prove up on a homestead, settlers were required to live on it for a certain number of months each year. The Lovewells fulfilled this requirement by living in their cabin to the West when it was safe, such as in winter. The rest of the time they still lived at the big cabin with the Davises.

Orel Jane and Josephine also stayed with the Davises while Tom was away in Junction City selling buffalo meat. There, while the Davises were away visiting the Fisher family, Orel Jane had another opportunity to prove her marksmanship. Wild turkeys, unable to find enough acorns, were eating from Dan's corn pile. Orel Jane laid her rifle on top of the rail fence, took careful aim and hit a big tom dead center through the neck. When the Davises returned home they were surprised to see the bird cooking on the stove. "It sure tasted good," she told Tom when he returned.

Tom brought back a copy of the *Junction City Daily*, which Orel Jane, always hungry for outside news, sat down at once to read. Suddenly she screamed and called Tom. "I know now what happened to Mary Ward. Did you read this article?"

She read aloud: "About two months after the capture of Mrs. Ward by the Indians, a woman that fit Mrs. Ward's description was seen by some soldiers, wandering alone on the Saline River. As they approached, she ran, apparently in great terror, into the timber. The soldiers, fearing a decoy, did not follow her."

"I just know that was her," she cried. Tom put his arm around her and tried to comfort her. "She was my midwife when Josephine was born and she was my very dear friend. Why can't we go find her?"

"Not much chance," Tom said. "That's many miles away and in very dangerous territory. I'm sorry."

SEVEN

Spring, 1868

Orel Jane, Tom, Dan and Mary peered into the midmorning sun one April morning as a dilapidated wagon with a shoddy canvas cover pulled up from the east. A young man and his very pregnant young wife sat on a straight board seat. They looked in need of a good meal. The man was dressed in a tattered Union Army uniform and a worn-out cap. His boots should have been discarded long ago. His black beard was in need of a washing and combing. His wife wasn't dressed much better. Her gingham dress was worn and dirty. Their horses were thin and haggard, reflecting their hard effort to get the young couple through rough and often muddy roads.

Inside the wagon the barest necessities were visible: an old table and one chair. Across his knees the man held a government-issue muzzle-loading rifle.

They stopped in front of the cabin. "Get down and come in," Tom said. "You look plum tuckered out."

"Ya sur air right about that, sir," the man said. "We're John and Florence Greenland from Illinois. I guess ya can see I'm a veteran of the late war. We've been travelin' for days, and we could use a stop and a cup of coffee."

"I'll fix you a bite to eat," Orel Jane offered, "I think you could use it." She went back inside the cabin and began to rattle pots and pans. She produced a sugar-cured buffalo ham and then began preparing biscuit dough. Tom helped unhitch the team and take them to the corral, where he gave them hay and a can of corn each. They ate like the hungry animals they were. "Let them rest awhile. Later we'll go up the valley to see what we find for a homestead," he added.

When they were finished with a big dinner and hitched up again, Orel Jane said, "You all come back after you've found what you want and stay here until the baby is born."

As they drove up White Rock Valley settlers could be seen busily building new log and sod homes and plowing sod. They were everywhere it seemed, and there were few sites left, especially along the creek. Wagons had been going by the Lovewells and Davises day after day, sometimes two or three a day. Tom hadn't noticed how many until now, and he realized good quarter sections were going fast.

"You may have to settle away from the creek, which means you may have to dig a well unless you want to haul water. I don't recommend you settle much farther west. Too much danger of Indians."

"We'll take whatever is available," Greenland said. "We'll have to hurry and get a crop in and a shelter built. I guess we'll live in the tent until we get that done. We have no money and we need garden stuff as soon as possible. I think I can get some wild game soon."

"We'll give you a sack of potatoes and buffalo meat," Tom offered. "Oh, thank you," Florence said, her voice full of relief.

"Talk about guts!" Tom muttered under his breath.

"What did ya say?"

"Nothing."

The Greenlands were typical of the new homesteaders coming in now. The first were generally people of some means; they had resources, such as money, with which to buy necessities. Those coming now were basically young people—often with young families—the majority of whom were Civil War veterans, both Southern and Northern. New homesteaders also came from the "Old Country," meaning Europe, or "back East," meaning any state east of Kansas. Many of them had little but their old wagon, a team of draft animals and their dreams.

They dug shelters in dirt banks, built makeshift sod houses or just lived in tents. If they didn't have stoves, they cooked outside over open fires. Tom warned them to be careful of fire as the tall prairie grass would burn easily.

So many men were busy farming and building homes that they again became negligent about watching for Indians. This negligence, combined with the knowledge that the Indian ponies hadn't yet regained their strength, led to carelessness. Tom tried to advise new settlers of the Indian threat, but with so many wagons coming through, he just didn't have time to stop and help everyone. The homesteaders needed to know how to protect themselves against Indian attacks, but while veterans knew all about guns, others, especially the Europeans, knew next to nothing about them. Tom found it difficult to teach them to use guns to protect themselves.

Whether or not the settlers acknowledged it, the Indian threat was real. For years the Indians had tolerated the cowboys, who trailed huge herds through to the northern markets. After all, the cow was merely the white man's buffalo, and the cowboys were nomadic, just as the Indians were. But the Indians resented the settlers slaughtering their favorite food supply, the buffalo, and their plowing of the luxurious grasses on which the buffalo fed. They especially resented the buffalo hunters, who were killing the animals just for their hides. The government encouraged this destruction, hoping to starve the Indians into subjugation.

The buffalo was important to the Indian in so many ways. It was the perfect commissary: besides high-quality meat, the buffalo furnished hides for tents, robes that kept them warm in winter, clothing, sewing sinew and bones for tools.

Buffalo roamed the country in uncounted numbers from Mexico to Canada; estimates varied from ten million to more than 500 million head. There were four main herds that moved north in spring and south in the fall within certain circumscribed limits. When the herds moved north they formed a dense mass, often a mile wide, stampeding as they went, razing anyone or anything in their path. No one understood their hurry. They were known to have jammed up against railroad trains, derailing locomotives and cars. When they reached their favorite grazing grounds they spread out in smaller, more evenly numbered herds, which helped to prevent overgrazing. Here they bred and gave birth.

***

One evening in late May Tom plopped down in the chair that Orel Jane had shot a hole through. He surveyed the country. The soil was just as rich as Tom thought it would be when he dug that hole so many years ago. The corn stood six inches high, and Orel Jane's garden was popping up. Green grass covered the hills and the flat country to the north. Rain was plentiful and the prospects for a bountiful harvest never looked brighter.

"Just look at that stuff grow," he said to Orel Jane and Josephine, who had joined him in the shade of a huge cottonwood. "Your vegetables will soon be ready to eat."

"Well, it will be good to have something fresh from the garden to go with our cured meat," she replied, darning a sock. Josephine played with a rag doll Orel Jane had made.

Life in White Rock Valley seemed like heaven, and for once, Tom was content to settle down and create a home for his wife and daughter. From his vantage point, he could hear and see neighbors tending their homesteads and he could watch his cattle graze north of the creek on the best grass in the world.

Tom's herd had grown. He bought longhorns from the trail herds and calves from settlers who needed money. He hired neighbor boys to herd. They would take the cattle out in the morning and corral them near home at night. Orel Jane worried that the boys might be attacked by Indians. So did Tom, but it was a necessary chance he had to take if he was to build a herd. The natives seemed to be fairly quiet this spring but it was too early to be sure.

The next morning Tom looked up from his work on the corral to see a huge cloud rising south of Round Mound. Orel Jane, seeing the cloud at the same time, came running from the garden with Josephine in her arms. "Tornado!" she yelled.

"Buffalo!" Tom said. "Get in the house."

Orel Jane ran into the house with Josephine and lay her on the bed, then came out to see the sight. The cloud of dust grew larger and larger and ahead of it came the buffalo, heads low, shoulders bobbing in unison, the earth rumbling under thousands of hooves. "Well anyway, it sounds like a tornado," Orel Jane shouted.

They ran back into the house to observe from the window and watch the large animals come across the yard, bumping into the protruding logs of the house, shaking the house until Tom and Orel Jane were sure it might come tumbling down. Clouds of choking dust crept into the house and Josephine cried out in fear.

After what seemed like hours the herd finally passed, churning up White Rock Creek and moving north over the hills and out of sight. Everything outside the cabin was in ruins. The new corral was scattered all over, posts broken off. The cornfield and garden were absolutely bare and rock solid.

"Look at my garden!" Orel Jane cried.

"Look at my cornfield!" Tom said. "We'll have to plant it over."

He rounded up the mules, which had raced east to dodge the rampaging herd, and spent most of the day rounding up the cattle. One cow was so badly injured that he had to shoot her.

One buffalo cow that was trampled as the herd crossed the creek remained there, unable to move. Tom carried corn to her and some hay. She ate the hay but nibbled on the corn, unsure of what it was. Tom fed and cared for the cow all summer, and by fall she had recovered enough to rejoin the herd when it headed south.

***

"Now is the time to watch for Indians," Tom said one morning as he was leaving to hoe weeds in his young cornfield. "Their ponies are nice and fat." Orel Jane took note. Every day she scanned the nearby hills, the creek banks and the cottonwood grove. "When nothing happens, people just get careless," Orel Jane thought. Indians were masters at the quiet approach. Just turn your back and there they were. She took the binoculars and scanned the hills, including the top of Round Mound. Warriors had been seen on top of this mound on several occasions, standing straight as a statue and motionless, then disappearing so quickly one hardly knew they had been there.

Early in June a newcomer came by and stayed the night. The next morning Tom took him up the valley to show him around. At mid-morning Mary Davis came by for a visit. She and Daniel had just returned the day before from a visit with his mother in Clyde. The women were so busy visiting that they forgot to watch for Indians and didn't see three ride up from the south. Orel Jane spotted them just as they slid off their mounts. She stood in the doorway, rifle in hand. Mary crawled under the bed. "No use doing that, Mary. Anyway, what would we do with Josephine?" Orel Jane said.

The Indians paused a moment to survey Orel Jane and her rifle, then proceeded. The men were bare except for the usual breech clout, which they weren't too modest about keeping in place. Their hair was braided and hung down both sides of their head, making them appear more effeminate than they really were. Orel Jane remembered one soldier who had passed through the area remarking that Indian men looked more like women and that the squaws likely were stronger than the braves since they did all the work. He claimed that the men laid around or took long rides to visit or pester homesteaders. "How could you improve on that system?" he laughed.

One of the intruders had a piece of embroidery around his neck. Orel Jane wondered if it had belonged to Mrs. Ward. As they reached the door Orel Jane stepped back to let them in. The Indians—she thought they were Sioux—sat down along the wall, and one immediately said, "Bread." Indians loved white women's bread; it was always their first demand when they came into a settler's home. One of the Indians glanced at a basket of kittens in the corner.

The three sat down against the wall, legs crossed, waiting but not speaking a word. They refused Orel Jane's invitation of a seat at the table.

As Orel Jane knew, not all Indians were on the warpath; many stopped at farmhouses for a taste of the white woman's homemade bread, especially that made from whole wheat flour.

With this in mind, she laid her rifle across the warming oven, got out a bowl and mixed up some corn bread. She stirred up the fire and baked the bread on top of the stove in a skillet, at the same time keeping a wary eye on the unwelcome guests and her baby. She put Josephine in her crib and told her to stay there. Mary crawled from under the bed and sat on a chair, still wearing a worried look on her face. Josephine went to sleep.

When the bread was ready she served it into the Indians cupped hands. They gulped it down and demanded more. Orel Jane shook her head and said no and they got up to leave. The leader again looked at the kittens as if to pick them up. Instead he tucked Josephine, who began to kick and scream, under his arm. He flipped a leg over his pony's back and rode off.

Horrified, but determined to remain calm, Orel Jane remembered Tom telling her how Indians liked to swap. She picked up the basket of kittens and ran after them, yelling "Swap you, swap you!" The Indian looked at the kittens, then at the kicking Josephine, as if not quite sure what to do. Finally, maybe thinking kittens might be easier to handle than a squalling child, he swapped with Orel Jane. She held Josephine especially close as the Indians rode away, stopping a short distance ahead. Still recovering from her scare, she watched in horror as the Indian killed the kittens before crossing the creek and riding south.

"That's what they would have done to our child if we hadn't swapped, I am sure of that," Orel Jane said as she told Tom of the incident when he returned. "And that embroidery around his neck—I am sure it belonged to Mary Ward."

She shuddered as she was reminded once again of the article that appeared in the *Junction City Daily*, a copy of which a passing settler had left with them in gratitude for their dinner.

***

Gomer Davies was a young settler and new neighbor of the Lovewells. Living with him was his ten-year-old sister, Mavis. Their parents had died of typhoid fever as they drove west. When Gomer was busy in the fields, Mavis was apt to come over and visit Orel Jane. They became close friends.

Mavis was a pretty child, full of vigor and vitality. She thoroughly enjoyed life on the plains and her visits with Orel Jane. Orel Jane enjoyed her too, treating her like a daughter. She helped Orel Jane with the work and played with Josephine by the hour. Other times she would run out on the prairie and among the trees, looking for small animals and birds despite Orel Jane's admonition to stay near the cabin for fear of Indians.

Mavis had a bar of soap and thoroughly enjoyed going down to the creek to bathe. One day as she was lathering her hands and face and enjoying her daily toiletry, she was completely unaware of two Indians watching from behind a tree on the north side of the stream. She was singing "Oh, Susanna!" at the top of her voice but stopped short when she saw the two Indians cross the stream and ride up to her. She screamed at the top of her voice as they approached, grabbed the bar of soap from her and began rubbing their dirty bodies and faces with it. They laughed and whooped and paid little attention to Mavis at first. Then one of them stopped abruptly, snatched her by the waist and mounted his horse, dropping the bar of soap on the creek bank.

Orel Jane, hearing the commotion, came running, rifle in hand. Seeing the bar of soap on the bank she picked it up and ran after the men shouting "Swap you, swap you!" The Indian stopped, dropped Mavis and took the bar of soap in hands already well lathered. They laughed gleefully as they rode away, rubbing their bodies with soap. This was a surprise to Orel Jane, who thought that Indians had little use for soap and water. Orel Jane held Mavis in her arms as the child cried uncontrollably.

"See what I mean," Orel Jane admonished

"Yes, I see what you mean. I'm sorry. I will be more careful."

***

No matter what the settlers did, from planting corn to building a house, working together was a common practice. It gave the men a chance to work together, visit, and protect themselves from Indian surprises. In August, Tom, Daniel Davis, Gordon Winbigler and Don Lewis began a group haying effort. They began up north and worked their way toward White Rock Creek. One man mowed, another raked and the other two hauled the hay home on a hay wagon. The grasses—bluestem, switch and Indian—were at their best.

Working in grasses that were often six feet tall made it hard to watch for the wily red man. The settlers carried guns with them and stashed more in the wagon box. Sometimes, when there had been no Indian troubles for a while, the men became lax. There hadn't been much trouble lately—except for the episode with Mavis Davies and a few isolated requests for food. Still, Tom kept watching instinctively. "It's the ones you don't see that get you," he told himself. They could approach so quietly, hide behind the smallest bush and lie in hiding without moving for hours.

The tribes were still determined to drive white men from the country west of the Republican River. But they had no intention of fighting the white man's way. They could see no point in coming out in the open when they could fire from ambush with little threat to their own necks. They were more bold and more open if they attacked in number.

Each day the hay crew moved toward the creek; today they were near its banks. Most of the men were near the creek, mowing and raking. Tom was north on a knoll, loading hay mowed the day before, when he saw about eighty Indians. Practically hidden by trees and grass, they crossed the creek eighty rods west of the crew. He shouted and waved his arms to the men and fired a shot into the air.

The element of surprise gone, the Indians raced toward the hay crew. Tom did likewise, jumping on his wagon and speeding to the crew. He barely gave them time to catch hold of the wagon as he circled and raced to the Davis-Lovewell cabin, the community fort in times of trouble. The mules were no match for the fleet Indian ponies and the red men were soon on their tails, firing an arrow now and then. The men rode in the back of the wagon, using the end gate as a sort of a wall, firing at the approaching braves. Neither they nor the Indians hit anything. A bouncing wagon made a very poor target for the Indians and an even poorer shooting position for the haymakers.

Winbigler, a new immigrant, always wore a stovepipe hat that he had purchased in New York when he got off the ship. He was very proud of it; maybe too proud. Although it never stayed on in a high wind, he wore it everywhere. He was used to chasing his hat, so when it bounced off he jumped off to retrieve it. He picked it up and tried to catch the wagon but the Indians were too close and Tom didn't dare stop. An Indian drove a lance through Winbigler's back, pinning him to the ground. As he rode past he reached down, picked up the hat and jammed it down on his own head. Lewis shot a hole through it, knocking it off, which was the best shot of the whole trip. The brave whirled and retrieved it.

77

Tom whirled the team in front of the cabin; the men jumped off and ran inside. There Orel Jane had her carbine poked through a porthole, firing at the Indians and keeping them at a distance.

Tom and Lewis, stationed on each side of the cabin, resumed firing at the circling warriors, and Orel Jane ran ammunition for them. Daniel stood back, still refusing to fire a gun. The circling men exhibited their best horsemanship, lying along the side of their horses and firing arrows from underneath their animals' neck, reducing the settlers' targets.

Tom, with his long-range rifle, shot a horse from under a warrior, but he jumped on behind another rider and kept on going. Toward evening they let go with a few war whoops, waved their arms in derision and rode south and out of sight behind Round Mound. "Let's see if Winbigler is still alive," Lewis suggested.

"Not a chance, but we can check," Tom said.

They found the man in a pool of blood, scalped. Lewis broke the lance in two and pulled it from Winbigler's body. Daniel officiated at his funeral the next day. As was his custom he read a portion of a psalm, gave a short eulogy and ended with prayer. White Rock Cemetery was filling much too rapidly and few of the dead died of natural causes.

After this episode, the settlers were called to a meeting at the cabin. "We've got to do something to protect ourselves," Tom said. "Custer is in the western part of the state doing what he can to bring the Indians to terms and onto reservations, but he can't do it all."

"I don't believe these renegades are from a certain tribe. I think they're what're called 'dog soldiers.' They are outlaw gangs, responsible to no one. Most of them are said to be Cheyenne, but men join from other tribes too. According to Custer, the name came from 'chien,' the French word for dog, hence the name dog soldiers. They are never satisfied unless they are at war with the white man. He says they infest most of the upper Republican and Solomon River valleys and that means us.

Lewis suggested that they build a fort. After a vote, the settlers decided to build a fort ten miles up the creek from the Lovewells, stock it with food and water, and station guards there day and night. They built it with lumber hauled from Daniel Davis's new two-story water-powered sawmill he had constructed along White Rock Creek. The upper floor was built cater-corner from the lower floor so that one could see all around.

78

There were portholes on all sides, on both levels. Around it, they also built a stockade. At Tom's suggestion, two flour barrels were filled with water and buckets were placed nearby. A stack of hay was placed in one corner so people could feed their horses in the fort.

"A favorite trick of the Indians is to fire a flaming arrow onto the roof or onto the haystack, which starts a fire and forces those inside to run out," Tom warned. "We should keep the hay in a place where the Indians' arrows can't reach it, or where it won't do any harm if it burns."

A man was to be stationed on a hill to the south where he could view the whole surroundings. He was to fire two shots—to let settlers know it was not someone shooting game—in the air as a warning if he saw Indians around. Everyone who heard the shots was to rush to the new fort, Fort Holmwood, if they lived nearby or run to the Davis-Lovewell cabin.

After the fort was built, Tom, Adam Rosenberg, James Reed and Robert Watson from Lake Sibley went hunting. They hadn't seen Indians for some time, and it was time to put in a winter meat supply.

"Pretty risky," Orel Jane said.

"It's a chance we have to take," Tom said.

They chose to go north, up near the Republican River Valley and north of the new fort. They found a small herd in the valley south of the river. They approached from the leeward side and had shot one animal when Tom, always alert, saw about thirty Indians coming over a hill north of the river, riding south at full tilt. They were fully five miles distant but they were approaching fast.

"Dog soldiers," Tom said. "They have the fastest and toughest horses."

"Jump in the wagon and let's go!" Watson shouted.

"Naw, let's shoot 'em up," Rosenberg offered.

"We would lose either way," Reed replied.

"Reed is right," Tom countered, watching nervously through field glasses. "But we're running out of time. How about if Watson and Rosenberg take the wagon up the draw there while Reed and I try to decoy them away. When they are out of your sight, head for Fort Holmwood."

It was not to the men's liking, but the situation called for desperate action. The warriors were now crossing the river and a little out of sight. When they appeared again, Tom and Reed wanted the Indians to see them running east near the bluffs. As Tom had hoped, the riders took after them, waving their lances, whooping with their worst war cries.

When the Indians dropped from sight again, Tom and Reed dropped down in the tall grass. They lay down, rifles ready to fire at the first Indian to appear. The Indians rode wildly past and Reed shuddered at the sound and sight. When the coast was clear, Tom and Reed jumped out and ran up a draw to the south. Both men were tall and long legged and they ran for dear life. Huffing and puffing they stopped on a ridge.

"I guess we fooled them, didn't we?" Reed asked. They had to stop for a good laugh as well as to catch their breath.

"They'll be back soon looking for us," Tom cautioned. "Let's go—maybe we can slow down a bit. And maybe catch the wagon," he panted.

The men in the wagon waited in a long coulee, watching for Reed and Tom. When the two appeared, Watson and Rosenberg turned and raced their team back to pick them up, then raced toward the fort. They stayed there until after dark, when each returned home.

"Let's go huntin' south tomorrow," Rosenberg suggested as they separated. "Well, why not?" Watson asked.

Tom and Reed were not so sure it would be safe, but they agreed.

The next day they drove over the southern bluffs and through Switzer's Gap, a deep, well-timbered draw. They saw what looked like buffalo about five miles away and started that direction. They hid the wagon in a grove of trees and left two men in charge. Tom and Reed went to find the buffalo and make the kill. When the men heard the shots they were to bring the wagon that direction. Reed and Tom quickly discovered that what they thought were buffalo were actually Indians. The Indians discovered them at the same time and started riding toward them.

There was no chance of escape this time. Tom and Reed ran back over a hill and hid in the tall grass. The Indians, knowing they were somewhere around, scoured the hills and draws all around them, jabbering in their language all the while. Once they were so close the men could almost touch them. They lay flat, guns ready for a last-ditch stand. Finally the Indians gave up and rode south.

After dusk Reed and Tom hurried back to the wagon, where the other two men were sure glad to see them.

"Ve tout tey got ya for sure," Rosenberg said, with his heavy Norwegian accent. "Ve could see tem lookin' for ya."

"Don't see how we can get buffalo if all we run into are Indians. Let's go home," Reed said.

The next day they went north again with greater success. This time they got all the meat they wanted without being bothered by unfriendly Indians.

***

Fall, 1868

Come fall Tom heard of a large herd of buffalo to the south, near the new Jewell City. He and Orel Jane went to visit Daniel and Mary Davis at the big cabin. The Lovewells had moved back into their own home four miles west of the original cabin.

"We could get our winter supply and take a load of meat to Junction City," Tom said.

"Let's all go," Orel Jane suggested. "We can leave the children with neighbors."

The Davises now had four children. Daniel was reluctant and he still didn't want to use a gun.

"Oh, come on. We all need the meat," Tom urged.

"I have this feeling we'll regret it."

Tom won the argument. They left the children with friends at Scandia. It seemed to be safer there on the east side of the river. They then drove south ten miles, crossing the river just above the mouth of Buffalo Creek. There they were joined by a party of six young men in a spring wagon also going west to hunt buffalo. They were in high spirits, drinking and having a good time.

The two groups traveled together for some time, but the men seemed more comfortable with their own company. In the afternoon the Lovewells and Davises decided to veer off to the north and away from the young men. Later the six were joined by two men in a wagon pulled by oxen. The Lovewells kept them in sight until evening.

The next morning both groups continued west. Sometimes they could see each other among the hills and draws, sometimes not. That night the Lovewell party camped four miles northwest of Jewell City; the other party camped four miles west of the village.

No buffalo had yet been seen. "Wonder where they are? There are plenty of signs," Tom mused as Orel Jane and Mary prepared dinner behind the wagon end gate. "I'll go over the ridge there and see if I can see any."

Orel Jane was busy frying buffalo steak when she thought she heard someone call loudly. She didn't understand so she called back, but there was no reply. "I suppose it's Tom," she said to Mary, "probably saw buffalo," and went back to getting dinner. Then she saw a wagon going over the ridge and thought it was some of the other party that might have found the same buffalo and wanted to get in on the kill. She never thought of Indian trouble.

Tom came back for dinner. Shots rang out as they ate. "Sounds like they found game of some kind. I can hear them yelling at each other." he remarked.

Daniel and Tom looked for buffalo that afternoon to the south and west but found none. Luckless, they returned home via Scandia.

Some time later, when several residents of Cloud County learned that their friends hadn't returned from their buffalo hunt, they organized a search party and asked Tom and Daniel to help. There were a dozen men in the party, heavily armed and wary of Indians. A man was sent to the top of the ridge in either direction as they rode along to look for signs of the warriors. They followed a bloody trail from west of Jewell City to the remains of the hunters' wagons; what they found told the story fully. In their fury the Indians cut up the harnesses and broke up the wagons. The search party found a violin bow that had apparently been used as a bow for arrows. A whiskey bottle was broken over a wheel.

"Must have been quite a party while it lasted," a search party member said.

Daniel picked up the bottleneck with a disapproving look. "Too drunk to hit anything. We haven't found a dead Indian, but there's a lot of blood in the buggy box. Too bad."

Following the wheel tracks, it appeared the Indians attacked the six men with the light team and buggy four miles west of Jewell City just as they began to hunt. It was a running fight from then on. Two miles east they were joined by the Collins Brothers with a yoke of oxen and wagon. Indians killed the oxen, and the Collins apparently jumped in with the other six in the buggy.

The running fight continued east to near the crossing of West Buffalo Creek. The hunters, believing the Indians were waiting in ambush near this crossing, turned and drove south. They turned east about a mile and a half south and from then on it was a furious battle. One man, who had been killed by this time, lay in the box. The rest fired from the box as the driver followed the ridge east. By now the horses were fagged and could no longer run. The Indians surrounded the hunters, shot the horses and killed the men on the spot.

Toward evening, the party had lost hope of finding the victims and agreed to go home. Suddenly they found the bodies, which were in such a bad state that all they could do was shudder.

"All we can do is bury them right here for now," Daniel suggest. "Later we can give them a proper burial in the cemetery. I could hold a brief ceremony."

Daniel quickly performed the ceremony; the burial was equally brief. Dan hurriedly quoted "ashes to ashes, dust to dust" adding a quick prayer. They shoveled a little dirt over the bodies and piled stones on top of it, hoping wild animals would leave them alone but knowing full well they wouldn't. As they made their way they found the broken violin. "Indians probably played with it until they tired of it and discarded it," Tom said.

When Orel Jane later learned of the tragedy that occurred that day, she said "Thank you, God, for your protection and for taking such good care of us." Tom added "Amen" as he looked out the door with his famous faraway look.

***

Despite the tragedy at Jewell City, White Rock Valley remained relatively calm, at least temporarily. Tom, Orel Jane, and Josephine stayed in their new cabin, and Simpson Grant was born there on January 23, 1869. Tom wanted him named after his good friend General Ulysses Simpson Grant. Both he and Grant grew up in Ohio. Orel Jane was assisted by Mrs. W.R. Charles, a new immigrant from Wales.

Like so many others, the Charles family had stopped at the Lovewells for information about settling in the valley and other advice. Tom and Orel Jane were always interested in folks who came from the "Old Country," especially England, their ancestral home. The Charles came with three sons and two daughters.

"We first settled in Pennsylvania, where I worked in a coal mine," Charles said. "But we thought it a poor place to raise a family so we came west to settle in this White Rock Valley."

"Tom will help you get settled here. He always helps people find homestead sites," Orel Jane said.

The two families hit it off well right from the start. Charles had much to learn about the West and he was a willing pupil. His Welsh accent and clothes stood in sharp contrast to Tom and Orel Jane's frontier garb. The next day, while the women discussed homes, schools and family, Charles and Tom drove up the valley. Tom pointed out the good grass and the good soil. Charles, however didn't seem to be as interested in farming as most men were.

"I would rather go into business," he said, "have a store and sell machinery and stuff."

"We could use a good store," Tom answered. "We have to go too many miles to get what we need."

Tom and Charles began to talk of laying out a town. White Rock City, as they called it, would have stores, banks, a livery stable, a church and a school. They planned to add the Colony House as a refuge for those running from Indians.

The St. Louis newspaper Charles brought confirmed that Indians were still a threat. It included a front-page story of a battle between General Custer and the Indian tribes in southwest Kansas. Tom read it with much interest, for the reporter left out none of the gory details.

In essence, the article reported that Custer had had so little success fighting Indians their way that he decided to bring them to terms his way, attacking in winter while they were camped and their horses were getting thin on poor winter grazing.

He waited for the most difficult moment—for both the Indians and his men—to attack. During a winter storm that broke loose in late November, dumping a foot of snow and bringing bitter cold, he selected his soldiers. The best shots mounted their best horses and marched toward an Indian camp in the Washita Valley. The attack was a perfect surprise to the chiefs, who never supposed Custer would be so daring. The camp was surrounded and attacked at daylight. Many warriors escaped the first onslaught, ran into the woods and exacted a high price on Custer's men.

Custer captured many women and children and burned the village. He didn't know there were other villages further down the valley and was surprised to see hundreds of warriors on a hill above him, waiting for his next move, ready to attack. Custer's men rounded up more than 800 Indian horses near the camp. It was a desperate moment, yet he still hesitated to do what he did: he shot nearly 700 Indian horses, saving only enough for the women and children who were captured.

The slaughter was a severe blow to the warriors on the hill but they weren't ready to quit yet. Frightfully outnumbered Custer decided the only way out was to fake a start toward the other villages. The warriors, fearful for their camp, circled and rode to protect their tribes. When they did this Custer and his men, as well as the captured women and children, returned to Camp Supply. Custer called it the Battle of the Washita.

The article concluded that Custer's report to his headquarters ended on a high note, but he regretted the loss of nineteen enlisted men and Major Joel Elliott and Captain Louis M. Hamilton, two valuable leaders. Custer assessed the outcome of the battle: "103 warriors were killed, including Chief Black Kettle; the capture of fifty-three squaws and children, 875 ponies, 1123 buffalo robes and skins, 535 pounds of powder, 1050 pounds of lead, 4,000 arrows, 700 pounds of tobacco." He also attested to the complete destruction of the village.

"Custer insists his only purpose in fighting the tribes was to bring them to the peace table and force them to agree to stop killing settlers and capturing and torturing their wives and children," Tom said. "But every Indian knows the government wants them on reservations and out of the way. This may be a terrible blow to them but it is not the end of our troubles. The Indians are fighting for their last stronghold and their way of life."

EIGHT

Spring, 1869

Tom stood looking at a tall, straight cedar tree in the hills southwest of his homestead. Now that the Lovewells had finally moved back into their own cabin, Tom would add corrals and a barn. He looked to the treetops to check their length. Then he looked off to the south and west for signs of any unfriendly warriors. He didn't look expecting to see a person—Indians were too smart for that. Instead he watched for birds in the treetops suddenly making an unusual racket, a raccoon chattering up high or a squirrel racing to a treetop. He saw no such telltale signs.

Selecting poles was getting harder now. Homesteaders cut trees for cabins and corrals, too, and the tree line was receding much too rapidly to suit Tom.

Tom kept talking to himself as he surveyed the trees. "Let's see. I'll need the posts first, then I'll come back for the poles. For the posts the trees must be a foot or more in diameter. Then I'll have something large enough so that I can cut holes in it for smaller poles. I'll need at least three poles, maybe four, to make a corral five or six feet high, which will keep the longhorns from jumping over. Or, I could buy a roll of that new barbed wire and put one strand of that on top of the posts."

He took another look at the distant trees in the dark forest, checked his rifle again and stood it against a small tree. Only then did he begin sawing at the base of a suitable tree. When he had a load down and trimmed he pulled his team in close and cut two poles for rolling the logs onto the wagon running gears. When loaded he sat on a stump to rest. He looked around at the dense trees to the south and west once more. Their beauty reminded him of the trees at the head of the American River in California where he found his stock of gold.

When he arrived in California back in the fall of 1849, he was more than surprised to find the gold fields well taken over by diggers. He reasoned: "If there is so much gold in the valley here, there must be a mother lode higher up." As he predicted, he found a rich sand bar at the head of the river. When that sand bar petered out and he was ready to go back down he was approached by a haggard looking man who said he had just come from Death Valley. His partners had died there and he had barely escaped. He wanted six men to return with him to claim the gold he had discovered there. If they would put up forty dollars each, he would furnish a map.

It seemed like a good thing and the map looked authentic. Tom found five other men willing and able to claim the gold, all of whom gave the man forty dollars each. The man promptly disappeared, but the six decided to go anyway. Deep in the desert, they ran out of water in the intense heat. One night, when they were about to die of thirst, Tom scouted and found a spring. One man perished when he drank too much at one time. The party never found gold, just an old anvil. But Tom was fond of reminiscing about those days and he shared the story with anyone who would listen.

Snapping back from his daydreaming, Tom loaded the wagon and returned home. They had built the cabin three years earlier but hesitated to move because of Indian scares, but Tom thought the scares would soon be over. Homesteaders pouring in daily would overrun the Indians with their sheer numbers. It was as if the settlers believed the country was a vacuum; they thought of it as uninhabited and free to be settled—which they did. Already the valley was nearly filled with people; settlers were homesteading the hill country away from White Rock Valley too.

At home, he unloaded the logs and cut them to the desired lengths. Using a heavy chisel he cut large holes in the logs and set them in the ground in a large circle. He went back for small poles, which he tapered and fitted into the holes in the posts. When he finished days later, he had the herder bring the cattle into the corral for the night. There would be no more night herding now except when he felt there was danger of an Indian attack.

***

On a trip to Junction City, Tom visited his cronies at Fort Riley. It had become a custom for those already called old-timers to get together and reminisce. Orel Jane always went with him when she could, but this time, with Simpson Grant so small, she stayed home. While there he purchased a fine Morgan stallion, a two-year-old cavalry colt, and named him Black Morgan. His coat was coal black except for a small white star on his forehead. He was of the finest Morgan stock. Tom had always loved fine horseflesh, and he decided that this was the time to do something about it. Black Morgan would breed with mares throughout the valley. Soon there would be many fine saddle and driving horses in the neighborhood, all sired by Black Morgan.

Tom turned him loose in the corral. There he would watch for hours as Black Morgan raced around, nostrils bulging, head high, his black hide glistening in the sun. His shrill whinny could be heard miles away. Tom also bought the finest cowboy saddle he could find. Each day he saddled up Black Morgan to get him used to it before the day when he would break him to ride. Each day he would reward the horse with a handful of corn or oats. It was one of Tom's finest moments and Orel Jane was there with him, her usual black dress whipping in the breeze, calico scarf on her head, Simpson Grant in her arms and Josephine at her side. Black Morgan would run up to the fence, snort in feigned fear, then return to his race with the wind. He was a fine specimen and Tom showed him off to anyone who came by, especially Charles, who had the same love for good horses.

One day Tom rode back quickly from a trip up the valley. He noted an ominous cloud in the west-northwest speeding east. He put Black Morgan in the corral and came to the house to warn Orel Jane that they should prepare for a bad storm. It started to rain just as he came in.

It rained and rained, by the bucketfuls for nearly an hour, dumping more than five inches. Such a storm was known as a cloudburst. "The creek will flood," Tom warned, "and if it does we will be in trouble."

White Rock Creek flowed outside of its banks frequently and often came close to the house and barn. "This time it will be worse," he said.

During the wet spring the creek rose a little higher each day. White Rock Creek dipped south just north of the cabin and the stream had trouble making the turn, so it overflowed south, coming near the house some days.

Tom built a dike around the house, scooping dirt from each side of the dike. He made the dike higher and higher, until it was four feet high, yet the rising water nearly kept up with him. Neighbors had the same trouble. Some of them merely moved to higher ground and let the water flood the houses and carry away whatever was loose. Orel Jane helped Tom tar the wagon box, anticipating having to float out. He tied Black Morgan south on a ridge. Water lapped over the edge of the dike before it began to recede. The flood had its benefits, though. The water left enough driftwood in its wake to supply the settlers with next winter's fuel supply.

***

Word came that the Indians, including the Pawnee, had renewed their vow that no white men would settle west of the Republican River, especially in the White Rock Valley, as it was near one of their former tribal homes. Many years before they had been visited by Spanish conquistadors who presented them with a Spanish flag and signed a treaty giving them perpetual rights to the White Rock Valley.

Orel Jane said one day at the breakfast table, "One can't blame them for fighting for their homeland."

"No, we can't blame them," Tom answered. "I don't know the answer. The government has tried to stop the settlers, but how do you stop ants marching across a field. We have never treated them right and we have broken every treaty we've made with them. Now we steal their land one bit at a time. I have always gotten along with them fairly well, although I would never trust one; they are all liars."

"They have a healthy respect for your marksmanship. But you have never fired unless fired upon," Orel Jane added.

The Indians in the area were already agitated, but what stirred them up the most was the deliberate killing of an Indian child near Scandia. Indian children were playing around a prairie dog town one day when some white ruffians, drinking liquor, came near and started shooting at them, killing one. The Indians demanded that the scoundrels be turned over to them. Either the Scandia people couldn't find them or they refused to turn them over to the Indians, knowing that they would be submitted to the cruelest torture. The ruffians insisted they were just trying to see how close they could come without hitting a child, a lousy excuse.

An Indian war followed. The White Rock settlers renewed their vigil, stationing men at both Fort Holmwood and at the old Fort Lookout. Men were stationed on hills to the north and south. The Indians began taking revenge on settlers both south and west of the Republican River.

Anna Frazer came by the Lovewell-Davis cabin to see about finding a farm that was not too far out and not in too much danger from Indians. "I'm a widow but I have Buckskin, this Irishman, to help me. He's a good boy though a bit of a talker," she said.

"Land is pretty well taken up around here," Tom informed her. "I've heard there is a quarter-section three miles east of here for rent if that would do. You would be near us, and there's a cabin already built."

"That sounds just like what I am looking for. I'll go see the landlord. Who is he?"

"I'll give you his address. You can write him."

One day, not long after Anna rented the farm, Robert Watson, who lived across on the next quarter-section was busy plowing. Busy watching his plow, he failed to notice Indians riding between the house and him. Anna saw the Indians and realized they had Watson completely cut off, apparently aiming to kill him and capture her. But Anna had other ideas. She came out with her double-barreled shotgun and fired at the Indians, reloading and firing again as she ran toward Watson's cabin. She did little damage to the Indians, but she scared them into riding far enough away to allow Watson to unhitch his horses and ride one of them to his cabin. Inside the cabin he grabbed his Winchester, then ran to the doorway and joined Anna. They continued firing as the Indians crossed the creek and rode north out of sight.

***

Soon after Anna and Watson's scare, seven men stopped at the Lovewell cabin to inquire where they could find buffalo. Some of them, including Burke and Wenkespeekle, gave their names and said that they had come from New York City to Waterville. John McChesney, a young settler, had been hired as their guide.

"I think up near the Republican River would be a good place to hunt," Tom said. "But look out for Indians. They are on the warpath. In fact, I recommend you don't go at all."

"We can handle 'em," Burke said, his bravado enhanced by the liquor he was drinking. He brought out a jug and offered Tom a drink, which he refused. "We got Spencer rifles and plenty of ammunition," he added.

"Those are famous last words when it comes to Indians," Tom said.

They crossed the creek and went northwest. Tom was hitching a span of mules with which to finish planting corn when he heard rifle shots. He climbed the corral fence for a better look and saw Indians riding hard toward the river. Surely, he thought, those men were not foolish enough to fire on those Indians. But there was no game in sight.

Late the next day McChesney was back with a party.

"Tom, would you help us bury the bodies of the hunters?"

"What happened?"

"These men lacked experience with Indians and were out for a good time as you noticed yesterday. I tried to stop Burke from shooting at the Indians when we left here but he wouldn't listen. I told him they would be back even though they were well out of rifle range. The Indians rode out of sight quickly. I said we better go back; the Indians will find us. They just laughed. 'We scared 'em off didn't we.' One of them laughed.

"I said Indians don't play that way. They went on and I went with them against my better judgment.

"We found a herd near the Nebraska state line and killed enough animals to fill both wagons in a short time. When we came back they insisted on camping on the west side of the river near White Rock Creek, even though I urged them to camp east of the river. I was sure the Indians would be back.

"The next morning I got up before daybreak and hid in willows along the river and watched for the Indians. Sure enough they struck at dawn, tomahawks in hand. The men made a run for it but the Indians shot them or tomahawked them before they got to the river. After they left I sneaked down the river to Scandia, wading or swimming, just keeping my nose above water. The brush kept tearing my clothes and my hide until I was bleeding. I was almost naked when I got to Scandia and bleeding all over. I got some clothes at the first house I saw then went to town to find someone to help me bury the dead."

Tom rounded up Charles and other men to help with the burials. McChesney led them to the site and found the bodies near the river. Some had arrows stuck in them, some were badly mutilated. "He's the one who took a shot at the Indians," McChesney said, pointing to one of the bodies.

The wagons loaded with meat were still here, but the horses and the camp supplies were gone. Harnesses were cut into foot-long pieces and one of the rifle barrels was bent around a wheel spoke.

"I'm hungry. Let's cut off some meat and cook it for dinner," one said.

"Wait," Tom cautioned. He cut off a piece and gave it to one of the dogs. He wolfed it down and almost immediately went into convulsions. In a few minutes he was dead. "Poisoned," he added.

"How?"

"We don't know. Some say they mix up a potion and pour it over the meat."

*****

One morning Adam Rosenberg, a relatively new settler who Tom had hunted with before, stopped by the Lovewells. In his broken English, flavored by his heavy Norwegian accent, he explained to Tom that he was anxious to settle permanently in the area. "Ay yust want to find a gud farm and hunt buffalo. Ay got rifles and farm stuff."

Tom looked in his dilapidated wagon and saw two old rifles. "I'll help you find some land after we have breakfast."

Adam was naïve about the west. Tom tried to enlighten him, without much success. When they had found a homestead up the valley quite a ways, Adam came back to help Tom build his new corrals. After that Tom helped him find good, straight cottonwoods for a house and helped him build it.

They soon became good friends. Adam couldn't wait to go buffalo hunting again. "Ay yust want to shoot one."

It was a dangerous time to go hunting and though he promised Adam they would go, he kept putting it off.

Finally, after corn planting, Adam and Tom hitched up a span of mules and headed up the valley to hunt buffalo. Adam put his rifles in the wagon box, but Tom paid little attention to them. They swung south from Fort Holmwood, which had been renamed Fort Walker. Tom left Adam with the team and crawled to the top of the next ridge. There he carefully scanned the region with his field glasses. When he was satisfied there were no Indians waiting, they proceeded to the next ridge; Tom scrutinized every nearby grove of trees carefully. But Indians were perfectionists at hiding, never making a move or wiggling a tree branch.

Adam was getting nervous but he waited patiently for Tom to return. His rifle lay across his lap, ready. Tom, on his trip to the next ridge, spotted a herd in a small valley.

"You watch the team while I sneak up on them," Tom said. He hadn't gone far when he saw three Indians riding hard towards Adam. He turned and ran back but before he could get close enough to help Adam he saw an Indian fall off his horse. The others stopped long enough to reach down, grab his rifle and ride on. Back at the wagon he asked Adam if he had seen any Indians.

"Ya yust better pet ay did!"

"Did you shoot at them?"

"Ya yust better pet ay did. Ay yust took gud aim and fired."

"Well, there's a dead Indian in the ravine over there. I saw him tumble off his horse as I came back but I didn't hear your shot."

They went back to investigate. There lay the Indian with a bullet through his heart. Adam apparently had fired just as the three rode over the ridge and didn't see him fall. Adam was beside himself. He danced around the fallen enemy with glee. "Dat's gud, dat's gud," he yelled.

When they got back to the wagon Tom looked in the wagon box. There were two rifles in the box when they left home, one an eight-shot

Spencer carbine, the other an old single-shot Star. Adam, in his haste, had reached for the Star. He was furious with himself. "Tang, tang," was all he could say. "What if they had kept on a comin'. Ay cud haf shot two more Injuns."

"Might as well go home," Tom said.

"Why? Whose afraid of two tang Injuns?"

"I am. They're probably just over the hill waiting for us."

It was obvious that the Indian problem might still be much worse than anticipated. They were supposed to be headed for reservations, yet they were more deadly than ever.

On the way home Tom stopped at every cabin and arranged for a meeting at the Davis cabin the next day to organize a militia.

The next morning they sat around the big table while Mary and Orel Jane poured coffee.

Charles suggested they ask Governor James Harvey for aid. All agreed to that. "Tom, would you go?" Charles said.

The next day Tom rode to Topeka to meet with Governor Harvey.

"I think you're having more trouble with Indians than anywhere else in Kansas," Governor Harvey said. "I'll appoint Captain Richard Stanfield (a new settler and a Civil War veteran) to organize the militia. We'll furnish Spencer carbines, ammunition and rations, but you will have to furnish the men. Each will have to furnish his own horse and saddle."

At the next militia meeting sixty-five men volunteered. Stanfield issued guns, ammunition and standard army rations. He set up a rifle range near Round Mound and took time to train them in the use of the carbines, since many of them had never used one.

"Learn to use them as well as you can. Your life and the lives of your family may depend on it," he told them.

This time men were stationed at old Fort Lookout, south and east of White Rock on the hill, as well as Fort Walker, about ten miles west of White Rock. Lookouts were stationed at points north and south of the White Rock Valley too.

Fort Lookout was built some time around 1859. The two-story block house was built of logs, with the second story built cater-corner across from the first. There was a stockade all around, with a bastion on each corner. Everything was in disrepair and the militia went to work repairing it at once. It was manned on a twenty-four hour basis.

The renewed vigils gave settlers a false sense of security. Word spread that the Cheyenne and Arapaho tribes were on the warpath, but the information—believed to be merely rumor—was ignored. This oversight led to the death of one of Mr. and Mrs. Malcomb Granstead's young sons.

Malcomb Granstead sent his son to graze a herd of horses near Round Mound. The child didn't see Indians ride around the mound. After they ran off his horses, he ran toward the colony house, the place of refuge in White Rock City. But one of the Indians rode back and downed him with a rifle. The first shot felled the lad. He jumped up to run again but the Indian returned and shot him again, this time fatally.

Orel Jane, seeing this from her cabin window, reached for her carbine and ran after the lad. When she got there the Indians turned and fled. She gathered the lad in her arms and carried him to the Granstead homestead.

"They killed your son and ran off the horses," Orel Jane said as she presented the boy to his mother.

Mrs. Granstead hugged her son's body and cried for a long time. "Thank you so much, Orel Jane. I don't know what we would do without you and Tom."

The next day Daniel Davis conducted another funeral. The community was incensed over this needless killing. Some threatened to kill the next Indian they saw.

Indians stayed on the rampage, even the sometimes friendly Pawnee. One unconfirmed story suggested that a new settler, angry over the killing of the Granstead boy, shot an Indian woman who was nursing her child near a group of friendly Indians camped near the valley. This incident was thought to have started more rampages. Whatever the reason, trouble continued.

One morning Orel Jane heard a knock on the door. When she opened there stood three haggard men, so out of breath they could hardly talk.

"Seven of us went hunting up on Rose Creek near the Nebraska line. We left two men with the wagon while we went to find buffalo, and

96

when they heard us shooting they were to bring the wagon to us. Then we were attacked by Indians," one said. "We escaped but only because we were a mile away at the time. We could hear a lot of shooting so we know there was a big battle. There was no use going back so we came here for help."

Orel Jane hollered at Tom, who was working with Black Morgan. Sensing trouble, he put work bridles on four mules and led them to the cabin. "Here, jump on these mules and let's get a posse together first," Tom said, without waiting to hear their story.

Up the valley they picked up thirty members of the militia and rode north. They could see smoke rising in that direction. Along Rose Creek they found the wagon, burning, with carnage all around. After using blankets to put out the fire they found the bodies of two men in the wagon. The other two men were nowhere to be found. They had used the wagon box as a fort and the amount of spent cartridges indicated there had been quite a battle. Their rifles were gone.

"We may never know what happened to the other two men. They may have been captured," Tom said. "Let's get back and warn the settlers."

Along the way Indian heads popped up over ridges but none attacked. When they came in view of the valley they could see homes burning, indicating an attack had occurred while they were gone.

"Maybe the attack on the hunters was a ruse to pull us out of the valley," Tom suggested as they surveyed the damage. "We're going to find people killed."

Five miles up the creek, midway to Fort Walker, Peter Tanner's cabin was burned to the ground. As they approached cautiously, a man jumped from a bush and someone almost shot him.

"Don't shoot; it's me," he yelled as he ran forward. "The dang Injuns struck while you was gone. I ran into these bushes when I saw 'em comin'. I watched 'em ransack my cabin and set fire to it. When they was out of sight I shot off my gun to warn the settlers. I could see 'em run to the fort. But I'll bet some never made it."

The Indians had set fire to cabins as they rode down the valley. The militia found burned bodies in the cabins as they put out the flames.

Just as the men thought the Indian attack was over, they saw a party of horsemen ride over a distant ridge and disappear. The militia spread out and lay flat on the grass, rifles at the ready. When the riders reappeared, Tom yelled, "They're not Indians, they're white men. Don't shoot."

The men rode up quickly, unaware that they were in danger of being mistaken for Indians. One said, "We're from Salt Creek. We went hunting west of here and were chased off by Indians. We left our wagons hidden in a draw and we're going back to get them."

"Better not," Tom cautioned. "They've killed hunters up on the state line and you can see what they have done to these cabins."

The party took Tom's advice and rode back with the militia. Ahead they could see heads popping up every once in a while. Suspecting Indians, they gave chase only to find a group of Swedes, new immigrants who had just settled in the valley. They were scared out of their wits. "Ve go back to Scandia," they said.

The settlers stayed that night and several more at the forts. A few days later, thinking it was safe again, they began working together, rebuilding burned homes.

His corn planted, Tom continued to work with Black Morgan. His spirit and exuberance, combined with his gentleness, never failed to excite Tom. He was going to be the best saddle horse in the valley.

Three of the new Swedish homesteaders—Hunson, Haggeman and Burchlan—had moved back to the valley. They helped Pontas Ross plant corn in the newly broken prairie. Ross turned over layers of sod while the rest chopped holes and dropped in kernels of corn. They had stopped mid-morning for a rest some distance from the wagon where they had stashed rifles and revolvers. While they visited about the latest news they failed to watch for Indians.

Outside his barn, Tom saw Indians cross White Rock Creek and sneak up a draw in the direction of the corn planters. Quickly he grabbed for his rifle, telling Orel Jane to lock the door and get her gun. Then he rode up the creek to warn the men. He fired a warning shot into the air and yelled at the men to run back to the wagon. He saw an Indian head pop up over the ravine but drop back out of sight before he could fire. The next thing he knew about eighty warriors jumped out of the ravine and circled the men, who ran back to the wagon to pick up their rifles.

Tom held his rifle on one Indian, then another, without firing, letting them try to decide who would be killed first. They kept out of range. The badly frightened Burchlan was holding the team attached to the plow. "Tie the team to the wagon," Tom yelled. He stood there, stupefied.

"Tie up the team!" Tom yelled again.

Instead, the confused Burchlan slapped them with the lines. The team ran away, the plow stuck in the ground, broke the doubletrees and the horses ran free. The Indians surrounded the team and kept them in their midst. The battle continued all afternoon, the Indians firing, sometimes with rifles, sometimes arrows. The men fired back, never hitting the fast-moving targets, but keeping them out of range.

The battle, which began in mid-afternoon, lasted about three hours. Finally the Indians rode off, taking Ross's fine team of horses and their harnesses with them. Ross was furious over the loss. "I don't have any money to buy more," he stormed. "I'll just have to leave the valley."

"We're lucky that was the only loss," Tom consoled.

While the Indian problems continued, one group of settlers organized the Salt Creek Militia. Located south of White Rock Valley, they became independent of the valley militia. They built a small blockhouse for protection and they, too, stationed guards on hills and knolls around the fort. One member of that militia came by to tell Tom about their experiences with the Indians.

"One day our guards could see Indians sneaking around. The guards warned settlers to run to the blockhouse. They brought their livestock with them, including their milk cows. The Indians did attack, riding in circles around the fort, but not close enough to be hit by gunfire. Toward evening someone said 'We need help.'

" 'Why not write a note and attach it to the horn of my milk cow and turn her loose,' one man said. 'I just bought her two weeks ago from a farmer near Lake Sibley and she will try to go home.'

"The Indians didn't attack the next morning as expected. Later that day the settlers returned to their homes, while the man went in search of his milk cow. He finally found her, not at Lake Sibley, but contentedly grazing near Scandia.

"Scandia people saw her going by and captured her for their own, considering her long-overdue help from heaven. She was all milked out."

***

Travelers brought the Lovewells stories of more Indian attacks, which reportedly continued unabated from the Saline River on north and into Nebraska. Late that summer Tom and Charles, out hunting, found the bodies of the two slain hunters who had tried to outrun the Indians on foot. They took them back to the White Rock Cemetery for burial.

The Indians knew they were losing, but perhaps the deciding battle that forced the Cheyenne to leave the area was fought north and west of White Rock Valley.   In June, after numerous raids on settlers, the Nebraska governor sent out a cavalry regiment under General Eugene A. Carr, as well as three companies of Pawnee scouts under Colonel Frank North, to bring the Cheyenne to terms.

Although the Indians and the regiment fought several pitched battles in the valley, the army pursued the Indians for a couple of months without remarkable success. Finally the army surrounded them at Summit Springs in northeastern Colorado with horrible success. They killed the whole tribe, including the women and children. After that the Cheyenne left the Republican Valley, never to return.

NINE

Summer, 1870

As the Indian attacks continued, Captain Stanfield, the militia organizer, asked Governor Harvey for more soldiers. Harvey sent word that all he had available were new recruits. The rest of his national guard was busy trying to control Indians and protect settlers moving into western Kansas.

It looked as if the wars would never end. There were Indian attacks up and down the Republican valley, through western Nebraska and eastern Colorado. A band of Nebraska Pawnee, returning from a buffalo hunt in the south, was attacked by Sioux and slaughtered in a southwestern Nebraska canyon. General Custer was attacking—with limited success—wherever he found troublesome tribes.

Soldiers never really blamed the Indians. Buffalo were being killed by the thousands solely for their hides and settlers were swarming all over the plains. In retaliation, Indians killed settlers and scalped them or, worse yet, captured their wives and children and assaulted them. In return settlers shot Indians without cause. One bitter act led to another on both sides.

Governor Harvey was doing his best to protect the settlers. He asked Tom to lead settler trains across the plains to find the best homestead locations. Tom reported back that he thought things had quieted down and that the Indian troubles would soon be over, even though he was not so sure. He promised to let the governor know if aid was needed.

101

One day Tom saw a herd of elk off to the south. He had a hankering for elk meat and hides, and he wanted a bull elk head with huge antlers for a gun rack. He hitched up a span of mules and told Orel Jane he was going elk hunting. "I saw a large herd go over the hills south. They're spookier than buffalo so I might be gone a couple of days."

Orel Jane watched nervously as he disappeared around Round Mound. Five days later Chester Babcock, returning from Fort Riley, stopped at the Lovewell cabin.

"Where's Tom?"

"Elk hunting over south," Orel Jane replied. "But he has been gone most of a week and I'm worried that the Indians got him this time for sure."

"I'm worried about him, too. Soldiers out scouting reported that Indians attacked a wagon train coming up the Republican River, killing many of the travelers. The escorts who came back to Fort Riley said they saw 300 Indians heading west, about the same direction as Tom would have gone. I'll round up the militia and we'll look for him."

A few miles out the militia met Tom coming in with a full load of elk meat. "I trailed them for miles before I could sneak up on them," Tom said.

"The soldiers said they saw 300 Indians headed that way. Did you see them?" Babcock asked.

"Those dumb recruits probably saw that herd of elk and thought they were Indians."

Tom divided up his load of meat with the men and went home to tell Orel Jane about his hunting trip.

The next day Mrs. Charles stopped by to visit with Orel Jane. "Your husband sure was generous with that delicious elk meat."

"Yes, my husband is a very generous man. Many of the settlers had their first meal in the valley at out house. He's always willing to drop his own work to help someone find the best piece of land. When John Doxon's barn burned during a prairie fire, Tom took them a sow and seventeen pigs."

***

Each day Tom threw a saddle on Black Morgan and rode him around the corral until he was sure he was comfortable and used to having a heavy six-foot man on his back. Black Morgan enjoyed the rides—on command he would turn and cut back with the agility of a deer. Instead of a horse-and-rider relationship, it was a friendship; Black Morgan nickered shrilly whenever he saw Tom coming. One afternoon Tom rode him up the valley to show him off to his neighbors. Black Morgan was hesitant about leaving home; every twig that snapped along the trail spooked him. But coming home, he swung into a long easy lope that covered miles like a race horse, his silky black mane and tail flowing in the breeze.

He met W.R. Charles along the way, riding his dapple-dray saddle horse. "That's a fine specimen of horseflesh," Charles said. "Man, would the Indians ever like to get a hold of him."

"They better not. I'd shoot an Indian over this horse."

"I can't wait to have my mares bred to him."

Settlers waved from their fields and houses as the men rode by. Sometimes they stopped to pass the time of day. It seemed very quiet in the valley. No Indians had bothered them for some time. "Is it safe now?" a new settler asked.

"Let's hope so," Tom encouraged. He shouldn't have.

"These aren't the usual run-of-the-mill settlers," Tom said later, standing in the doorway and watching a half-dozen covered wagons come up the valley. All were pulled by the best draft horses, all evenly matched, four head to a wagon. Red paint on the wagon boxes contrasted with the white canvas covers. Kids played alongside; the ma's and pa's were perched on the cushioned seats, all smartly dressed in the latest fashions. When they pulled up in front of the Lovewell house Tom welcomed them in for a cup of coffee. Their leader, a tall man with a stovepipe hat, introduced the group. "We're professional people as well as farmers. We call ourselves the Excelsior Colony," he said.

Their wagons were heavily loaded with merchandise of every kind, from dress goods to the latest in farm machinery.

"I think I can show you what you're looking for," Tom said. "There's a community ten miles west of here called Holmwood."

Tom led them to Holmwood where they settled, taking over nearby Fort Walker. They quickly improved the fort to better protect against Indian attack. Soon they had built a thriving village.

That same year covered wagons with other well-to-do couples stopped at the Lovewell cabin to eat and inquire about the land. They, too, had families.

"We're Quakers," one man said. "We would like to settle with people of our kind and keep to our ways. We're looking for a community called Yorkville (known as Northbranch today)."

"I think I know what you're looking for," Tom replied. "There were Quakers there once. We call it Quaker Point. The land is good, it lays quite level and you can be by yourselves. But you have to watch for Indians. The first settlers moved out because of them."

"Sounds like the place we're looking for."

Tom and Black Morgan led them to the Yorkville community. There they found buildings that had been built by previous settlers in disrepair or burned. Grass and sunflowers, which do well after sod is broken, covered the street. It was not a pretty sight. The men wandered among the rubbish and weeds looking around carefully, talking it over in the quaint Quaker language interspersed with "thees" and "thous."

"This suits us just fine. More will follow from back East," the leader said. "We thank thee for being so helpful."

They set to work at once planning a community of fine stores to be built of lumber, not the usual homesteader's sod or logs. Farmers would live in town and drive out to their farms in the daytime, not from the European custom, really, but to protect their families from Indians.

Tom again advised caution in regard to the Indians, advising the settlers to come to Fort Walker if they could make it in case of attack. The new Quakers laid out plans for a settlement of twelve sections of land and sent word for friends to come.

Tom rode to Fort Walker and stopped to visit the guards. "Seen any signs of Indians?" Tom asked.

"None. Neither have the spotters on the hills. Been pretty quiet this summer."

"Maybe too quiet," Tom said, always leery when he didn't see signs of Indians.

***

Two months later Mr. and Mrs. David Wagner stopped and stayed overnight with the Lovewells. They also drove fine horses and were well dressed, their wagon loaded with muslin and gingham dress goods. "We got a message from the people at Yorkville and we want to start a store there," Mr. Wagner said. "Can you find us a guide?"

Tom rode with them for a several miles until he found a couple of young men the settlers could hire as guides. He checked the hills and scanned the skyline. When he saw no signs of Indians, he concluded it would be safe for them to go on to Yorkville. Tom rode home to get back to his haying.

He hadn't worked long before he saw the boys riding the Wagners' work horses his way, whipping them in a high gallop. When they got to Tom they were so scared and out of breath they could hardly talk.

"When we reached the Pontas Ross farm (Ross, the man who lost his team to the Indians in the fight in the cornfield, had moved back) on the narrows, where the creek comes near the hills, we saw Indians coming.

"We jumped down, unhitched the horses and jumped on their backs. The Wagners said, 'Where are you going?' We said, 'You get down in the wagon out of sight and we'll ride off to decoy them away from you. When they're out of sight chasing us, you run down to the creek and wade it to the Lovewell cabin. Keep low in the water, just keep your nose above water.'

"The Indians chased us as we expected, but we sure hope those people followed our instructions."

Tom sent a message the militia to the fort. From there they went looking for the Indians and the newcomers. The Indians disappeared but not before they had torn the canvas cover off the wagon and scattered dress goods all over the prairie. There was no sign of the Wagners. The militia hoped that they had taken the boys' advice and were sneaking down the river. When the men couldn't find them after searching the area and the creek thoroughly, they returned home.

The boy guides stayed that night with the Lovewells. Late that night one of the boys said, "I hear Indians whispering."

"Indians don't whisper," Tom said. "Let's go see."

Near White Rock Creek Tom saw figures running in the pale moonlight. Tom tried to catch up with them, yelling, "This is Tom Lovewell." The figures stopped. It was the Wagners. "We thought thee were those savages again," Mrs. Wagner said.

"Come in the house and get dried off," Tom said.

In the candlelight it was plain they were no longer the fancy dressed people who had passed that morning. Their clothes were in tatters, and they were shivering and bleeding from flesh wounds caused by tree limbs and brush along the creek. Mrs. Wagner was weeping uncontrollably.

Orel Jane brought out a pair of trousers for Mr. Wagner, a black dress for Mrs. Wagner, and stirred up the fire in the cookstove.

"We did just as thee lads told us," Mrs. Wagner said. "We kept underwater all the time and that is why the militia couldn't find us. We peeked up once and watched the savages destroy our wagon and goods."

The next morning, Tom offered to go to Yorkville with them but Wagner said, "No. We'll get our wagon and go back home. We've had all this pioneer life we can stand."

***

Shortly after the Wagners left, the Fort Riley commander agreed to send troops to White Rock Valley. They arrived a few days later, loaded with wagonfuls of supplies and hauling a cannon. They were green recruits from back East with no experience in fighting the wily red men. But they told Captain Stanfield and Tom they were ready to fight off savages and thought "it would be fun to fight Indians."

At least they were ambitious. The settlers watched them day after day as they dug dugouts in the bluffs south of White Rock Creek, digging them large enough to bring in their horses at night along with them. They made sorties up the valley, careful not to go too far. They grazed their horses out a ways, but keeping them in sight. They bought hay from the settlers, which at least improved the local economy. Otherwise, they lolled around their camp and made improvements such as pole corrals.

Meanwhile the Indians had grown ominously quiet again.

One morning while Tom Woodruff and Gus Heldt were cutting poles southwest of the Lovewells, they heard shouting west of them. At first they thought it was hunters coming, but it turned out to be Indians riding their way. They jumped on their wagon and raced to the Lovewell cabin, the Indians gaining all the way, firing arrows and guns as they came. Seeing the men coming in a cloud of dust with Indians right behind them, Tom stepped out with his rifle and started shooting. The Indians immediately pulled back and swung south, out of sight around Round Mound.

One of the Indians was wearing a white shirt, which told the men a settler had been killed, robbed or both. The settlers went to the soldiers for help, but the soldiers, instead of coming to help when they heard the shooting, holed up in their dugouts, their horses inside with them. Their captain all but refused to come out, but finally Tom convinced him he had to show his face, which he did reluctantly. The men saddled up, checked ammunition, got into formation and hooked up a team to pull the cannon. Captain Stanfield and the militia fumed at the delay. Finally, the soldiers followed Captain Stanfield, Tom, Heldt, and Woodruff. They checked with the settlers they passed as they went up the valley. Some said they had heard shooting but hadn't heard of trouble with Indians.

Soon, however, they found plenty of evidence that the Indians were nearby. At the farm of some new settlers several miles up the valley, the Peckhams, they found all five members of the family killed. Clothing was ripped off and Mr. Peckham's shirt was missing. The Indians broke up the furniture but didn't set fire to the house. "Just what I expected," Captain Stanfield said.

They put the bodies in a wagon to take them to the White Rock Cemetery for burial.

The militia held another meeting. They agreed they might as well send the recruits home. The recruits were only too glad to comply.

Two brothers, George C. and John Catlin, came to the valley, stopping at the Lovewells for coffee and conversation, as so many did. Orel Jane wasn't impressed with the two. She didn't pour coffee with her usual enthusiasm.

"We're challenging the homestead of the family killed by Indians," George said. "We don't feel good about it, but someone else will do it later if we don't."

"Let the blood dry up first," Orel Jane snapped. "We just buried the family."

Orel Jane's comments disturbed the men, but they moved into the house anyway. One day soon after a party of supposedly friendly Indians stopped by. They drank coffee and ate the Catlins' biscuits, then walked out to where John's team stood hitched to a plow. The Indians started to unhitch the horses.

"Leave the horses alone," George warned. They didn't, so he grabbed his carbine, took aim and wounded two of them. One took aim at the house with a shotgun. The shot peppered the door and one pellet hit his watch. The Indians mounted their ponies, picked up their wounded comrades and rode into the hills south.

The Catlins loaded their wagon and left the country, not even stopping to tell the Lovewells good-bye.

***

Tom left early one summer morning to check cattle south of Round Mound. Soon he was back. "I saw a herd of antelope over south. Maybe we'll have antelope steak for supper tonight," he said, taking down his Winchester.

"Be careful," Orel Jane warned. "There are still Indians out there, even though they never seem to bother you."

"I think the army has them under control now."

"Remember what you used to tell others, 'famous last words.'"

"I won't be gone long."

Black Morgan swung into an easy jog as they headed over the hill. Tom thought of Orel Jane's remark, which bothered him although he wasn't sure why. Would his luck desert him this time? True, he still had his scalp. He had never been so much as nicked by an arrow or bullet fired by an Indian. True, he had never fired unless provoked, and he was proud of the fact that he had killed few Indians outside of the time he spent with the army. They might respect him but he was never convinced that an Indian wouldn't have wanted his scalp hanging in his tipi or Black Morgan in his string. He respected them but didn't trust them.

Tom turned his thoughts back to the antelope. They seemed spooked, keeping just out of range as they moved south. Finally he rode down a draw west of them, tied Black Morgan to a tree and sneaked over the ridge, where he got a nice pronghorn buck in his sights. The buck fell near the edge of a creek and the herd ran on. Tom ran back to Black Morgan and rode to the fallen animal. There he cut the buck's throat, bled him out and began skinning. He was careful not to harm the head and antlers; this would be a fine trophy for his dining room.

He was leaning over gutting when something prompted him to rise. Just as he did, an Indian rose above the bank and fired an arrow, headed for the point just where Tom's head had been. Tom reared up and the arrow stuck in his knee cap. The Indian dropped out of sight. Slowly Tom limped to the small tree where his rifle stood. He put it to his shoulder, aiming carefully at the spot where the Indian had disappeared, sure he would try again. When the Indian peeked over the bank to check on the results of his efforts, Tom fired, striking him dead. The Indian let out a horrendous scream, rose high in the air and dropped back into the ravine.

Tom surveyed the country around for some time, sure there were more Indians around. Finally one came down a ravine a few rods away, riding south at full speed. Only when the Indian was out of sight did Tom take the time to check the arrow sticking from his knee cap, which was causing him intense pain. He gritted his teeth and gave it a mighty yank. He broke the arrow in two and threw it over the bank where the Indian lay.

He ignored the pain, finished skinning and dressing the animal, tied the carcass behind his saddle and rode home. He suffered as he never had before. But the red man's target was Tom's head, not his knee, so he was most grateful for whatever caused him to rise up at the right split second.

Back home Tom slid off Black Morgan and hobbled in the house to have Orel Jane remove the arrowhead and dress the wound. Orel Jane took one look at the wound and ran to get the laudanum and cloth dressings.

"Lie on the table," Orel Jane said, "so I can get a better look at it."

109

She looked the arrowhead over carefully and grimaced. She daubed it with laudanum. "I don't know; it looks pretty deep for me to extract. I may have to have help."

Tom stuck a .45 caliber bullet in his mouth and bit hard. She probed and dug until it finally emerged. The steel arrow was all but buried in his knee cap.

She helped him off the table to his rocking chair. "Oh, Tom, I always worried that they would get you sometime and I prayed for your protection. See, the Lord did protect you." She put her arms around him and hugged him once more.

"Well, anyway, that Indian won't bother us anymore," Tom said.

"There is no doubt that he had his eye on you and Black Morgan at the same time," Orel Jane said. "Your scalp in his lodge and Black Morgan in his herd would have become his prized possessions."

"Yeah, I've been very lucky," Tom added. "In fact, we have all been lucky. Let's hope the Indian troubles are over and we can live peaceably in this valley from now on."

***

Tom continued to fulfill his agreement with Fort Riley to guide groups of homesteaders through western Nebraska and western Kansas. Orel Jane and he discussed this often, and although it meant separation and danger for her and the children, she agreed that he should do it.

"The money will come in handy, I know," Tom argued, half to Orel Jane and half to himself. "But you'll be in danger."

"I'll be careful. If there is the slightest danger, I'll stay with Daniel and Mary. For $100 a month you'd better go. We can use the money. I'll hire neighbor boys to herd the cattle and tend the corn. Mary and I will come up and hoe in my garden."

Tom was called on often during the late '60s and early '70s. A trip would start with a homesteader's wagon train leaving Fort Riley and would usually wind up in western Kansas, western Nebraska or eastern Colorado. Along the way he might camp with Frank North and his Pawnee scouts. From them he obtained more valuable information on how to handle the wily Sioux and Cheyenne warriors. Sometimes Tom came home through Fort Kearney. Other times he came home through western Kansas, past Waconda Springs where he saw Indians come to get "spirit water." From there he cut north to Switzer's Gap and home to his valley.

His knee continued to give him trouble. It would slip out of joint and he would have to have help putting it back. Once, hunting alone, he stopped to get a drink from a small stream. His knee slipped out and he had to ride several miles in torture before he found someone to help reset it. Because of the natural jolting of his horse, the knee always caused him much pain during long rides.

Guiding a wagon train through central Kansas, Tom camped near a small stream. A small friendly Pawnee band that came from Nebraska to hunt camped across the stream. The squaws were busily dressing buffalo meat while the braves lolled around the fire, eating choice parts. As always Tom had the train make a circle for protection, though he felt there was no danger from these Indians. Both camps carried water from the stream and shouted greetings to each other. Children played on either side. They jumped in the stream and playfully splashed water on each other.

Along the way, two ruffians had joined the train. They drank and bothered the travelers and begged for meals. Tom didn't like the looks of them, yet he was reluctant to send them away; two people out alone still were not safe. Tom told them to either behave or leave. They agreed but soon were misbehaving again. Their language was offensive and they were quarrelsome. Tom's final warning went unheeded. "Tomorrow, you straighten up or you better be gone," Tom ordered. "And throw that whiskey away."

That evening the ruffians were still drinking and having a good time. They went over and sat near the bank of the stream, cursing the Indians on the other side. Their language was even more offensive than before. Tom lost his temper. They had rifles, but everyone carried a gun then, so Tom gave it no thought.

An Indian woman came down to the stream, dipping a bucket for water, and one of the men shot her dead. Tom marched over, cursing them roundly. "Why did you do that? We ought to hang you but the Indians will be over to take care of you better than we can."

111

Sure enough, the chief and three warriors came across the stream at once. "We want man who kill woman," the chief said.

"Is this him?" Tom asked, holding the man by the nape of his neck. "We fix him."

The wagon train leaders gathered around, hesitant to turn the man over, knowing how cruel the plains Indians could be if they were hurt needlessly.

"Then we start war," the chief said as he started back to camp.

"He means it," Tom cautioned. "If we don't give him up we'll all be killed."

Reluctantly, the men consented. The chief put a rope around the man's neck and led him back to the tribe's side of the creek, where he was subsequently killed. His cowardly partner disappeared back down the trail.

***

There was a message waiting for Tom when he got home. Would he be a scout for troops sent to fight a band of Indians that were killing and harassing settlers west of White Rock Valley? They had just massacred a wagon train and destroyed everything.

Tom consented, but when the troops arrived he wished he had turned down the request. The men were green troops, all blacks, sons of former slaves. Their commander, a white man, was no better trained and certainly not ready to fight Indians.

Forty miles out Tom picked up the trail of the tribe, numbering about 100, moving slowly. Tom ordered the men to travel only at night, make no fires and no unnecessary noise. As they followed the trail they came across children's toys and strips of calico dresses scattered along the way. Wagon covers were converted into tipis, their remnants left behind. The Indians—enjoying their ill-gotten gain—showed no evidence that they knew they were being followed.

It was a lark for the happy-go-lucky troops, who would lope their horses out in a wide circle and come back laughing and joking. Neither the commander nor Tom was able to control them. "Their antics will alert the Indians, and their horses will be so worn out they couldn't chase an Indian if they found one," Tom grumbled.

One morning Tom made an early morning foray and found tracks and evidence suggesting that the tribe was not far away. "They're just over that distant hill. Keep your men under control and ready to attack," he told the commander

The men settled down for most of the morning, that is until a jack rabbit jumped from under a bush. They took after it, whooping and hollering. When they got back their mounts were tuckered out. Tom was so angry he swore he would never be a government scout again. He rode ahead again to look but the tribe had disappeared down some of the draws and breaks and were nowhere to be found. The campsite, littered with food, clothing and a tent, showed they had left in a hurry.

"We'll just go home," Tom told the commander. "They're down there somewhere waiting for us and we wouldn't have a chance. Anyway, your horses are in no shape to do any running now."

Tom's next assignment was to guide a wagon train into Colorado. He rode down the Republican River to meet the train, where they would take a trail west. They took a circuitous route up the Solomon River through western Kansas and into eastern Colorado. After settling the settlers, the small group of soldiers and Tom returned through land neither he nor they were familiar with, believing it would be a time-saving shortcut. They thought they could live off the land, killing wild game. But there had been a severe drought and the game had sought better forage. In western Kansas they were getting desperate for food; Tom looked for meat of any kind.

He came upon a prairie dog town inhabited by thousands of rattlesnakes. Tom waded in, killing the big ones until he had a sackful. Back in camp he dumped the wiggly things on the ground and told the cook to skin and cook the meat. The cook went into shock and refused.

"Get those dang things out of here," he snorted, backing away.

"Aw, don't be so persnickety. Beats starving, doesn't it?" Tom asked as he began skinning snakes and slicing off pieces of meat into a kettle. Soon the hungry soldiers joined in the operation, while the cook hung the kettle over the fire gingerly. The troops ate the meat with relish, swearing that it tasted like fried chicken.

TEN

Indians didn't bother the valley much after 1870 except in friendly ways. Most were either on reservations or headed that way. Small tribes camped in the valley for a day or two, fished in the creek and sometimes begged for food. But the Indian tribe Orel Jane would remember best was one from Iowa that came to hunt buffalo, antelope and deer. Their chief brought with him his son-in-law and a few braves, who camped near Round Mound.

John Doxon and his wife came over for a visit one evening while the tribe was camped nearby. While they were there the chief came for a visit too. He acted peculiar; he would get all excited, then sing an Indian song or dance a war dance. Orel Jane, becoming more and more annoyed, finally whispered to Tom, "Get that old fool out of here."

"He'll be all right. Just too much fire water."

Orel Jane was not about to be put off with that remark. Tom was in the middle of recounting his trip to California years ago, which the chief continually interrupted. Finally, Orel Jane stomped her foot, and Tom took the hint.

"Maybe we can get him to bed in the attic, John," Tom said.

They struggled for an hour to get the overweight chief up the ladder. They might get him halfway, then he would tumble back. Finally the chief tried another vulgar song, after which he staggered out the door and found his way to a haystack near the corrals. There he whooped and sang all through the night.

The Doxons left and the Lovewells went to bed. "I never slept a wink all night," Orel Jane fumed the next morning as she prepared breakfast. Just then the chief came in, grinning sheepishly.

"If I did anything wrong, I pay for it," he said.

"No, you didn't do anything wrong," Tom replied. "Sit down and eat breakfast with us."

He talked for a long time, telling Orel Jane about his granddaughters, all named Josephine. Afterward Orel Jane said that was his way of apologizing.

C.S. Parker of Steuben came by a few days later and told Tom about his own amusing experience with some Indians.

"I was out in the field when an Indian came by and talked to my wife. She was frightened to death and hid the children under the bed when she saw him coming. He made all sorts of gestures while he spoke in his language and pointed to the cornfield to the south. When I came in, he started talking all over again. I finally figured out he was telling me my cows were in the cornfield. Have to say they're good Indians."

***

There was nothing Tom liked better than getting together with Samuel Morlan and his brother, Steve, and talking over old times. Of course, he still liked to talk things over with Orel Jane and make plans for the house, the farm, or whatever. He still liked to kid her about shooting holes in his buffalo hide chair. When they disagreed she flounced into the kitchen end of the cabin and rattled pots and pans; sometimes she would mix up bread dough. He enjoyed seeing her do that because her bread was second to none. He loved to cut off a slice of fresh bread and spread it thick with butter then sit back in his rocking chair and look out over the land, especially if he could see Black Morgan or some of his cattle in the distance.

One morning in 1871, Samuel and Tom sat around Orel Jane's kitchen table drinking coffee. It was during this gab session that the two men began to discuss starting a town just south of Tom's homestead. Tom had dreamed of this for years but never did anything about it. For one thing, they needed a post office. Their cabin had served as an unofficial one for years, with people dropping off letters to be mailed to distant states. Orel Jane would put them behind the clock high on the wall and away from the children for safekeeping. When a traveler came through he

115

was asked to deliver them to the first post office for forwarding. They needed a store that could handle the mail, so they met with Chester Babcock and asked him if he would sell some of his land, which lay just south of the Lovewells.

"How about forty acres and you pay my homestead fees?"

Tom now had a half-section of land just south of a bend in the creek and another quarter-section that joined it on the south.

"I'll furnish another forty acres from our land next to it," Tom offered. "Orel Jane wants to build a schoolhouse and church. We can put them on our land."

The four of them sat around the dining room table, spreading sheets of paper torn from Orel Jane's tablet on which they scratched designs for a village. Chester watched in fascination as he saw a portion of his 160 acres transformed into streets with stores, a school and a church.

"We should have two main streets," Morlan said. "One fifty yards east and west and one north and south."

"Sounds good to me," Tom agreed.

The next day the three men called on A.B. Gale, Ed Haney and A. Reynolds. All of them met at the Lovewell home and, again, sat around the table planning for more stores. Thus they planned the town and became the founding fathers.

"The next step would be to find a railroad willing to build through the valley and near this town," Tom said.

"That won't be a problem through this rich and well-settled valley," Morlan said.

"Yeah, but they always expect the town to put up money for it."

Orel Jane stood in the background, filling coffee cups. Occasionally she hinted at what she would like to see in a schoolhouse and church. The men listened politely and Tom suggested they get on with the details later.

***

Tom liked cattle better than farming and his herd expanded rapidly. His herd boys had to take them farther into the hills as

116

homesteaders ate up the prairie grassland. It hurt him to see it disappear under the plow. He had also gone back East and bought a couple of Durham bulls.

"They'll put more meat on than the Longhorns, and it'll be more tender. They'll also feed out at two years of age instead of the four to five years it takes for Longhorns," he explained to Orel Jane.

"Yeah, but what about the wolves. They'll kill those timid eastern cattle like tame deer," Orel Jane argued. "And they won't stand a hard winter."

"They'll make it all right. Times are changing. The Longhorns were fine for the open range and the long drive north. No other cattle could have made that 1500 mile trek and got there in good shape. In fact, some drovers could drive them to Montana and get them there fatter than when they left Texas. But their time is past."

The Morlans stopped by often when they weren't too busy. They were latecomers, but they were aggressive, hard-working men. Sometimes, if it was evening, they would talk most of the night. Orel Jane would go to bed and Tom would have to make coffee for the men.

The Morlans were members of the elite tribe of men who had made it rich in the gold fields of California. They took a ship around South America instead of going by covered wagon.

"We had no stomach for spending months on that trail," Sam said. "Because we sailed instead, we were in time to find good claims. We set up a store and made more money that way than panning for gold.

"We returned to New York by ship, uncertain what we would do," he continued. "We talked of going west, then heard of this valley from someone. We bought a covered wagon and teams and headed out. In Kentucky we bought a barrel of tobacco, thinking it might sell for a good profit out here. It sold well and now we're using that money for our businesses in White Rock City."

Although Tom had not been as successful as the Morlans, he still loved to reminisce about his adventures in California. He told the brothers how he had arrived in California late but had still managed to extract a small fortune from a sand bar by using his head and hunting upstream from where others had struck gold. He also told them of being taken by the swindler, and how he and five other men whom he had traveled with had nearly lost their lives in Death Valley. As he remembered the incident, every detail seemed fresh in his mind.

"We bought five burros and loaded them with supplies and plenty of canteens of water. At least we thought we had plenty. Soon after we got into Death Valley we noticed our water supply was going faster than we thought it should. We hadn't reckoned with the zero humidity and the heat. It was hot, boiling hot. When we checked the water bags carefully we knew we were going to run out of water soon. Some wanted to go back but we were too low on water for that; we could never make it. Going on and hoping to find a creek or spring was the only answer.

"We soon ran out of water. The burros died of thirst and we were soon to follow. Finally we lay down in the shade of an overhanging rock, ready to die. Our lips were swollen and parched. We were a sight to behold. We would have laughed at each other if it were not so serious. This would be our last night on earth barring a miracle.

"In the desert night, the air cooled and I revived a little. I looked at the pitiful men. I decided I might as well die walking, looking for water. I walked up a ravine and I thought I could smell water. The further I went the stronger the smell got. Suddenly there it was, a small spring bubbling up from the earth, flowing a little ways and disappearing in the sand.

"Was it a mirage? A trick of the mind? I flopped down in the cool water and took a small sip. I had been told, when starving for water, just take small sips and let the water flow throughout the body slow-like; otherwise, one could get cramps and die. I took a little more. I took off my clothes and flopped in the water and rubbed off some of the accumulated desert dirt. I did this for an hour or so, then filled my felt hat and returned to the men.

"I wet the lips of each man and finally aroused them. They mumbled and talked silly. I urged them to take a small sip. Soon they were on their feet and I told them where the spring was while still urging them to take just a little at a time and let it soak into their bodies. One of the boys was too far gone to make it on his own. And so I sent the rest on ahead and helped him. When we got there one of the boys lay on the ground writhing and screaming in pain. 'We couldn't stop him; he just lay down and drank,' said one of the boys. He was soon dead.

"We gave him a scant burial and covered him with rocks. We loaded our canteens and decided to do some prospecting anyway. We never found anything of value except some lead, which wasn't worth much at the time. We went east and came out in Nevada, where we bought a mine and worked it for a while until a severe winter drove us out. We sold out for $1,000 each so it wasn't all a loss."

***

Sam and Steve Morlan's store became the hub of the new village. It was situated on the corner, where each main street came together. The main entrance was on the south with a large porch. There was an entrance on the west side as well, facing the other main street. The store mainly sold groceries, trading for eggs and butter or whatever farm wives brought in. The eggs that couldn't be sold were tossed out back. The stench became overbearing sometimes, but there was no market for them.

When he wasn't farming or looking after his livestock, Tom stopped at the Morlan store to visit. There were chairs and benches around the pot-belly stove in the center and the cracker barrel stood nearby. A spittoon sat near the stove. Those who chewed tobacco—Tom didn't—could hit the spittoon from ten feet away. Some opened the stove door and spat in the stove. They wiped their mouths with their sleeves and hands, then reached into the cracker barrel for more crackers. A water bucket sat on a table with a dipper hung over the side.

There were many gatherings around the stove, and the political debates there often became heated. Tom vigorously defended his Republican party affiliation. There were homesteaders from the south who gathered around the stove and defended the Democratic party just as fiercely. The Civil War was refought again and again.

"You Yankees took away our constitutional rights and set our property free," fumed one Tennessean after he paused to spit an extra mouthful into the spittoon. "If you dang Yankees was going to do that you should 'av paid us for the slaves."

"Yeah, but you Democrats knew it was rebellion," Tom snorted, "President Lincoln freed the Negroes as an act of war. If you hadn't rebelled we might have helped send the blacks back to Africa or paid you to set them free. I saw Negroes sold in New Orleans and that was the worst thing I ever saw."

"Sure, that was the traders doing that. But we took good care of our slaves and treated 'em right."

And so the arguments continued whenever men gathered at the store. For the southerners "dang Yankee" was one word, just as "dang Democrat" was one word for Republicans.

Tom defended President Ulysses S. Grant with all the vigor he could muster. Both of them had grown up in Ohio and were good friends. When he signed up with the army in San Francisco he had hoped to be fighting slavery under the general's command, rather than fighting Indians along the West Coast.

While the rhetoric in the Morlans' store sometimes got political, more often the discussions were about the price of corn, cattle and hogs. Rain was plentiful and the prevailing theory was that rain followed the plow, in other words, "the more the land was plowed the more it would rain." They also discussed building the school and church, where they should be built and of what material.

The schoolhouse was built of stone hauled from Round Mound. It would be large enough for 100 students, and every bit of that room was needed. A stone mason supervised the stone-laying and did the critical work himself, chipping away here and breaking another there so that each fit properly. His profession fascinated Orel Jane, who supervised the schoolhouse herself. She saw to it that the planks for the students' seats were of good quality, without splinters, and that the teachers' desks were of top-quality walnut lumber. A big heating stove was placed in the center, surrounded by the student planks. The teachers' desks were to be in each end.

Orel Jane and Nellie Doxon became the first teachers, with more than 100 pupils by the end of the year. Together, they saw to it that important knowledge was properly implanted in all students, whether they were five, like Josephine, or sixty-five, like some of the foreign farmers. There were students who either didn't know the English language or had never learned to read and write. Students came from all over the valley, especially during the winter months when farm work was slack. Adam Rosenberg became one of the first students.

120

Daniel Davis supervised the construction of the church. He thought it should be about the same size as the school. "After all, it should be as important as a schoolhouse," he argued.

"Go ahead," Tom and Sam said. "Do whatever you like with it and we'll help build it."

Daniel, the carpenter in charge, elected to buy lumber from the sawmill. He personally constructed a pulpit of the best oak lumber and chiseled a cross on the front. A large stove was installed in the center with benches all around. The church was filled the first Sunday after completion. It was then that Daniel announced that he and Mary would not be the pastors for long; they had decided to sell their land, take a charge on the distant frontier, and serve the spiritual needs of those who were most needy and most lacking in facilities.

Businessmen built more stores, a livery stable, a millinery and, of course, a blacksmith shop, but no bank. A doctor set up office and advertised that he "didn't administer calomel." Businessmen wanted a newspaper but no printer seemed to be interested.

Ogle and Laney built a new sawmill in 1871, turning out "large amounts of lumber—oak, black walnut and cottonwood." It, too, was water-powered and located on White Rock Creek.

***

Horse thieves took the place of Indians as troublemakers after 1871. Tom was suspicious of Guy Whitmore and Jack Hanes when they moved into the valley near Salem, further west, and seemed to make a good living without doing much farming or anything else. "They'll bear watching," he told Morlan.

Soon the two men were beefing up their scant income by stealing neighbors' horses. They would, it appeared, sell them to settlers farther west. When it got too hot for them and they surmised that the neighbors were about to take them to court, they headed north. But the sheriff in Grand Island, Nebraska, who had been warned of their habits, arrested them when they came to town.

Jewell County Sheriff William Stone and Tom rode to Grand Island to bring them back. They caught them with illegal ownership of eleven local horses. Back in Salem, Stone left them in the custody of Deputy Jones. Jones had them handcuffed to a pole, sure they wouldn't leave when he had to run an errand. Tom went uptown to get a bite to eat.

But while he was gone, neighbors gathered up a mob, took the two men out and hanged them on the limb of a cottonwood tree. As a result, the county board wouldn't pay the reward to the sheriff because, they said, he didn't deliver the thieves "dead or alive" as required. Stone stormed out of the board meeting, madder than a hornet. Tom tried to argue with them too.

"You said 'dead or alive'—how could they be any deader than they are now?"

The board members still said "No." They claimed there was "little money in the treasury, and it was needed elsewhere," a lame excuse.

"We'll do what we can to see that you are never reelected," Stone threatened.

Another accused horse thief, Phil Baker of Holmwood, tried to kill John Gregory, then left the county before neighbors could bring him to trial. Stone put out a call to other county sheriffs but Baker was never caught. "He left for parts unknown," Tom told the sheriff after he had scoured the countryside around home.

Some horse thieves got away. But those who didn't were punished by hanging at the spreading cottonwood tree near Salem, which became known as the "hanging tree."

***

Adaline Lovewell was born August 16, 1872. Orel Jane was assisted by her good friend Nellie Doxon. White Rock Valley was settling fast, with a home on nearly every quarter section, maybe two if people took only eighty acres each. There was no room left for buffalo, which had moved into the hills outside the valley. They were getting fewer in number every day, as wagon after wagon loaded with buffalo hides passed by the Lovewells. The hides stunk, as did the hunters, and hundreds of carcasses of good meat rotted on the plains.

John Reihle, John Councilman and John Hawks, late arrivals in the valley, asked Tom one cold day where they could find buffalo. Tom

122

didn't encourage them; it was thirty degrees below zero with a foot of snow on the ground. "If you go, you will have to go a long way west."

"We need the meat," Reihle said.

They rigged a cover over their wagon and hitched a yoke of oxen to it. Tom loaned them several buffalo robes. They wrapped themselves in the robes and pulled out.

The next afternoon Councilman and Hawkes knocked on the door of the Lovewell cabin. They were on foot and shivering with cold. "Come in," said Tom. "But where's Reihle and your wagon?"

"We had trouble," replied Councilman. "We found a herd in the valley west of here. We left the oxen hitched to the wagon and sneaked up on the buffalo. But at the first shot the oxen ran away. We scattered out and hunted for them. We found the wagon about dark but no oxen. We couldn't find Reihle, either.

"The next day we looked for Reihle again and found him in a tree where he had spent the night. He was almost frozen. He had injured his foot on a sharp stick and could hardly walk. We made a tent of the wagon cover, wrapped him in the robes and walked home."

"You men get warm and I'll go after Reihle," Tom said.

A new arrival, Jim Kirkpatrick, who had stayed overnight with the Lovewells, offered his team and wagon. Tom loaded it with firewood and left. It was hard going in the deep snow and it was dark before he found Reihle.

"Am I glad to see you," Reihle said, his teeth chattering in spite of the robes and the tent. "I thought I would freeze to death last night."

Tom started a fire to get Reihle thawed out. He dressed his foot, which was badly injured from the pronged stick that had also pierced his boot. His feet were frostbitten and he screamed in pain as they thawed out. Tom cooked buffalo steaks for a meal before they wrapped up in robes for the night. Occasionally he put more wood on the fire during the night to ward off the bitter cold. It was still very cold when they returned home the next day.

The settlers' days of hunting buffalo were about over. The settlers and the hide hunters were about to exterminate the famous animal and furnish the final blow to the Indian tribes making their last stand for survival. The settlers would have to depend on their beef cattle for meat from now on; the Indians on a handout from the government.

Tom continued to expand both his cattle herd and his acreage. If a settler wanted to sell out, Tom was apt to buy his farm. He kept buying out settlers who wanted to move until he owned more than 900 acres, much of it grassland. He would never be fully convinced that the tall grass grazed or fed to cattle was not a better crop than grain.

ELEVEN

1874

Tom and Morlan sat around the cracker barrel visiting when a stranger walked in, bought tobacco and nibbled on some crackers. His cowboy garb—high-heeled boots, leather chaps, and wide-brimmed hat—stood out in high contrast to the overalls and straw hats of the farmers present. He also wore two ivory-handled Colt revolvers holstered on each hip. He walked with the stiff gait of a cowboy, his eyes trained to look for cattle on distant hills. Tom watched him with suspicion. He was too far east for the great herds; their shipping terminals were either at Dodge City in Kansas or North Platte or Ogallala in Nebraska.

Short of a low "howdy" he had little to say and offered no indication of where he might be headed. No one ever asked many questions of strangers.

No doubt he overheard Tom say he would have to ride to Hardy, Nebraska, that afternoon to withdraw money to pay the schoolteachers. Tom joked that Orel Jane needed the money for books and Nellie wanted hers for clothes.

Strangers often stopped at the store and normally attracted little attention, but when this man left Tom stepped out to watch him walk down the street. The stranger stopped at Steve's livery barn, which Steve operated along with helping at the store. Sam, who had joined Tom outside, asked if Tom knew him. "No, but I wonder about him. He looks like a hard character. Don't see many men carrying revolvers nowadays in this part of the country," Tom said.

125

Steve walked in and heard Tom and Sam speculating. "I wonder about that man, too. His horse is a tough mustang but it's been ridden hard. He had me give him an extra can of oats and a big feed of hay. He tried to trade horses with me but I said no. I'm sure he would have liked a fresh horse, but that one of his might be stolen."

Eventually the focus of the conversation shifted from the stranger to community problems, especially the chances of getting a railroad to build through White Rock City. Tom went home and, after dinner, rode Black Morgan to Hardy.

In Hardy, Tom, who never passed up a chance to visit with old friends, stayed at the bar and restaurant too long after withdrawing money from the bank. The sun was setting as he rode home. Black Morgan swung into his long, easy lope and it was dusk when he reached the bridge across White Rock Creek. As he approached the creek Black Morgan snorted and hesitated. Tom poked him in the ribs and spoke to him but he walked toward the bridge at a stilted pace, nostrils wide, head high. He jumped sideways when a man with a red bandanna over his face stepped from the shadows, clutched his bridle and poked a revolver in Tom's face.

"Give me that moneybag or I'll blow your brains out. And get off that horse!"

Tom didn't hesitate. But before he could hand over the money and dismount, Black Morgan grabbed the man's arm, threw him to the ground, whirled and raced across the bridge and galloped all the way home, sliding to a stop at the barn door.

At the barn Tom patted Black Morgan on the head and said, "Good old boy!" as he gave him an extra feed of oats and added a special pat on the neck. In the house he told Orel Jane about the incident. "That horse will never have to worry about me selling him. He will have a home as long as he lives."

Tom walked to Sam's store. Sure enough, the stranger had left late that evening with his tired horse. "He sure needed a fresh horse and Black Morgan would've filled the bill very well," Sam said.

The next day Tom called the vigilante committee together and they went looking for the outlaw. They inquired at several towns north and west in Kansas and Nebraska and sent telegrams to marshals and sheriffs, but without success. Some time later a federal marshal from

Dodge City stopped at the Lovewells and asked for a job. "I'm trailing an outlaw but I need money to continue," he said. "And I need a fresh horse. How about trading for that black horse of yours?"

"Never," Tom said, recounting his brush with an outlaw at the bridge. Comparing notes they decided he was the same man. The marshal worked a week, then rode north. Two weeks later he returned with the handcuffed outlaw. He stayed overnight with the Lovewells. "I'm taking him back to Dodge City for trial," he said. "He's wanted for horse stealing."

***

Trials and tribulations in the valley were not all caused by Indians, horse thieves or rampaging buffalo. Sometimes the land itself proved challenging.

In late July 1874, Tom went to work on his mower. "Cutting this prairie grass is almost like cutting barbed wire," he told Orel Jane. "Every week or two you have to overhaul the sickle bar."

The mower needed new ledger blades and replacing them was an aggravating job. The rivets were hard to drive out and Tom wondered if the hay was worth it. But it was needed in winter, for if the snow blew and piled in drifts, the cattle could no longer graze.

"Just be glad you have it to mow," Orel Jane suggested unsympathetically. "You want Black Morgan to go hungry?"

Times were good in the valley. With the exception of an occasional drought, crops were good each year. While much of the corn burned up in the heat, there was usually a fair wheat crop and sufficient grass and hay. Settlers prospered and built new homes. Even Orel Jane hinted to Tom that they could use a larger home "what with their growing family and all."

Around Morlan's cracker barrel there was more debate about the rain following the plow theory. Tom said maybe it was true, but Morlan said the weather records prove it. "They don't call this the Great American Desert anymore, do they? Just look at the rain this year."

That year rain was more than adequate: the wheat crop was excellent and corn never looked more promising. Oats and barley waved knee-high in the wind and ripened with golden colors.

Martin Dahl bought a new threshing machine and paid for it by threshing for the neighbors. It was true he almost lost it in the river when he got stuck crossing. Tom had to round up several span of mules to help pull it across.

"Never saw a year look better," he said as he thanked Tom for his assistance.

"It's a wonderful valley, just as I said many years ago." Little did Tom know how soon things would change.

The morning of the disaster started much like any other day. Orel Jane poked the fire in her stove, prepared two pie crusts and filled them with gooseberries, freshly picked. Then she kneaded a batch of bread dough and set it on the back of the stove to rise. Josephine, rag doll in hand, and Simpson Grant played in the yard, pretending to be farmers and raking the fine dust. Orel Jane baked the pies and set one of them on the window sill to cool. She noticed the children playing in the dirt and stepped out to scold them for getting dirty when she noticed a huge cloud coming suddenly from the south. "Tom, come in right away. There is a big storm coming. You children get in the house at once."

There was no thunder or lightning. At first, thinking it was a bad storm approaching, Tom came and helped Orel Jane get the children in the house.

But it was no storm. Soon the land and the sky were black with grasshoppers. The sky turned hazy from the flying mob, which ate everything in sight. Tom's corn and Orel Jane's garden disappeared in minutes—they ate the leaves off the trees and the clothes off the line too. The pie Orel Jane had placed in the window to cool disappeared down the throats of hungry insects. They crawled into the houses and chewed on anything they could find.

When they left a day or so later to feed on crops farther north of the valley they left a barren desert behind—no crops, no grass, no leaves on trees. They even ate the tuber roots deep in the ground. It was a disaster for White Rock Valley. Fortunate were those few who had planted and harvested wheat earlier—they would have flour for bread.

There was no grass left for the cattle, and, if one had not already put up hay, there would be no winter feed.

Wagon after wagon loaded with destitute and discouraged homesteaders passed the Lovewell home, bound for their relatives or anywhere there might be employment.

One family stopped at the Lovewells. The husband had scribbled in large letters across the side of the wagon cover, "Goin' home to my wife's folks."

"Much obliged for helping us get started this spring but we can't stay. We ain't got no food and no clothes for the children," he said over coffee.

"We have some garden stuff stored but it won't do much good among so many," Orel Jane said.

"Maybe we could get relatives and friends back East to send us stuff," Tom suggested. "Let's call a meeting."

As usual, when there was a problem, the solution was to call a meeting. Settlers, especially new settlers, gathered at the Lovewells.

"We were totally dependent on a new crop, especially garden stuff," one said. "Now we have nothing. It's no use."

A lot of ideas were kicked about. "Why not send someone back East to gather up supplies and food?" one said.

"Sure, why not," Orel Jane answered, passing Tom's big hat. Men chipped in quarters and dimes and then elected Jackson Peters to make a trip to Ohio. He had a good covered wagon and good mules. Two months later he returned with sacks of beans and clothing. Martin Dahl helped distribute the supplies but refused to take any for himself. He said he had a good wheat crop and didn't need any.

Tom and Orel Jane also turned down help. "We have food stored in our cave; we don't need much," Orel Jane said. "We'll get by."

Folks back East heard of the disaster and responded. They loaded boxcars with food and clothing and dropped them off at the nearest railroad east of the Republican River. Wagons were sent to pick up the items.

To new settlers with nothing in reserve and little money, those loads of food and clothing, picked up from the boxcars, were a blessing form heaven. There were many unusually dressed people that winter,

129

some wearing Amish hats and Quakers pants, a few even sporting stovepipe hats. Peters insisted Dahl take home a sackful of beans anyway, and Dahl shared his wheat.

The Lovewells survived the devastation and welcomed their fourth child, Stephen Rhodes, who was born December 7, 1874.

***

In 1875, the Otoe Tribe, some 500 strong, crossed the Republican River and White Rock Creek and camped a few miles west of the Lovewells. It would be the last tribe to camp in the valley. They created a lot of interest and some nervousness, especially among those who had seen the depredations of earlier Indians. But there was no trouble. The Otoe showed off their brightly decorated horses, their painted faces and the feathers in their hair. A few young bucks raced their steeds out among the settlers, laughed at the children and called them "paleface papooses."

***

On October 12, 1878, William Frank was born. Again Orel Jane was assisted by Nellie Doxon. Both had retired from teaching in White Rock City but remained bosom friends for life.

"It was this year," Orel Jane wrote, "when I learned that 'God is in the Wind.' My infant son William Frank was cross and fussy. I was up trying to rock him to sleep when it seemed that the night had grown ominously quiet. I stepped to the door and looked out. To my horror, a tornado was tearing its way toward the house and was but a short distance away. It was such an awesome sight that I stood spellbound, losing the precious minutes I had left in which to warn the family. All the while I stood there I prayed that God would spare us. Then suddenly a cold wind, as from a hail storm, hit and the tornado raised just over the housetop. I whispered a silent 'Thank You, God.' I was assured that God is everywhere—even in the wind."

During that same year, Rose Hill School, named for the profusion of wild roses which grew there, was built by Andrew Shirley, with the assistance of Paul Dahl and Charley Smith. Tom furnished his stone boat. The school was large—twenty by thirty feet—large enough for the thirty students who attended. As soon as it was built, children began scratching their names and initials into the soft limestone. The rosebushes flourished and students brought the teacher bouquets.

George R. Thacker built a water-powered flour mill with a turbine wheel and three runs of stones—two for wheat and one for corn.

As the White Rock area continued to grow, so did the need for a local source of printed news. Morlan and Tom continued to talk of the need for a newspaper, hoping a printer would move in. "Sure we know all the news around here but we need a record of it," Morlan said.

"And we need something to read," Tom added. He had become an avid reader after learning fully from Orel Jane.

As if in answer to their wishes, H.E. Taylor drove into town one day, stopped at the store, and offered to bring in printing equipment. Morlan found an empty building just down the street, which Taylor furnished with a printing press and hand-set type. He published the first issue of the *White Rock Independent*, a weekly, on April 11, 1879. The front page featured the usual "boiler plate" used by most small weeklies; inside there were many local items.

Tom took a copy of the White Rock City's first newspaper home and read every word to Orel Jane while she prepared supper. "Just listen to this: Dr. Clark Johnson has an ad for his Indian blood syrup, 'the best medicine known to man.' He says he has thermaline, a remedy for ague, Graefenberg pills for headaches, biliousness and fevers. That ought to take care of our aches and pains."

"Well, it ought to cure or kill," was Orel Jane's skeptical reply.

He read on. " 'For Sale: A farm of 160 acres, ninety acres under cultivation, orchard of young trees, grove, two wells and plenty of water, a good house, etc. – J.Z. Scott, M.D., White Rock, Kansas.' And, 'For Sale: One colt, coming two, one wagon, a stubble plow, one double shovel cultivator, one harrow, twelve and one-half acres of timberland. About three miles northeast of White Rock; one-fourth interest in a cultivator. Call Dr. Forsha, White Rock, Kansas.' Harvey Parian's large ad offers 'horse blankets very cheap and heavy all-wool double ladies' shawls, and breakfast shawls.'

"And listen to this one," he gloated. " 'Mr. T. Lovewell has hundreds of bushels of seed corn and has a sample in his house a foot high. Out of fifty-nine grains there were only three seeds that didn't grow.'"

Both Tom and Orel Jane laughed over an item in the August 15, 1879, issue that quoted another regional paper, the *Herald*: " 'A gentleman in Salina who owns two farms is about to engage in a new line of business. Having a large crop of corn, he intends to market the corn and cut the stalks up into cord wood, calculating to have about twenty cords of wood, which would be clear profit.'"

Advertisements in the paper ran the gamut. There were ads for Chicago Pitts threshers; doctors, including M. Mosena, physician, surgeon and obstetrician; and P. McMutchon, counselor and attorney at law. Businesses bought space too, including Keagy and Low, carpenters and builders; William Smeck, wagon and carriage specialist; Miss E. Cleland, milliner; F. O. Crouch, dealer in watches and clocks; Schuler and Leigh; Levi Hays, blacksmithing; George G. Smith, harnesses, saddles, whips, fly nets and collars. S.E. And S.R. Morlan advertised dry goods and groceries in their general store.

Browsing through the ads, Tom said to Orel, "Guess I'll go to Miss Cleland and buy you a new bonnet."

"Huh," Orel Jane snorted.

Tom also read a long article about the Fourth of July celebration that the Lovewells and almost every other settler for miles around attended. " 'There was a full day of programs ending with a dance at the Magnificent Canvass Bowery, where they remained until near morning. Everything about the ball was well conducted and pleasant. Perfect order was maintained throughout the entire evening. The dance was borne along by the excellent string band music and by the perfect organ accompaniment of Mr. Will Haver.'"

There was a fireworks display at 1 a.m. The editor added: "But the complete absence of liquor, which the character of public opinion of the town compelled, was sufficient guarantee of good order.

White Rock City became a beautiful village with a population of 250. The storefronts were painted in a variety of colors: blue, green and red. Homes were small, well kept and usually painted white, with gardens in back. The town was neat for the most part, with the exception of the junk thrown about in front and behind the blacksmith shops. The discarded eggs behind the Morlans' store were sometimes an eyesore—they still got more than they could sell—but local cats and dogs frequently ate the garbage, which helped keep the smell under control.

As more and more strangers passed through White Rock City on their way West, the city began to need a hotel. Mr. and Mrs. Tippery built and operated the Happy Hollow Hotel and served the "finest meals." It was a favorite stopping place for peddlers and traveling men, who went out of their way to stay there overnight.

Talk of a railroad through town surfaced whenever the town fathers met at the store to gossip and discuss other subjects. "We sure could use a railroad," Sam Morlan commented. "It's a nuisance to have to haul in all our goods. We need a passenger train." Tom and the rest agreed. "Maybe we should have a meeting," he added.

The *White Rock Independent* reported that George Thacker bought a forty-horsepower steam engine, which was installed by Fred Cooper, so that the mill could be kept running during periods of low water in White Rock Creek, which usually occurred in August and September. It also indicated that with the breakup of the water-holding prairie sod, water no longer flowed into the creek as steadily as it once did.

The local school still flourished, although Orel Jane and Nellie Doxon no longer taught there. The *Independent* noted that the average number of students was fifty-eight, while the average daily attendance was forty-nine.

The newspaper ended with the December 26, 1879, issue. Taylor didn't say why he quit, he just told Tom the grass was "greener elsewhere" as he hauled out a case of hand-set type.

Tom hurried back to the store to have a confab with Sam Morlan. Both returned to the printer. "This is a surprise to us. We thought we were supporting you well. What is it?" Sam asked.

"Just say maybe I got a better offer," he replied sullenly.

"Just a typical sour-mouthed printer," Sam said as they walked back to the store. "Hope we can find another one who's better."

***

133

One day a well-dressed gentleman in a cutter, pulled by a fine team of Morgans, drove into town and stopped at the Morlan store.

"I represent the Chicago, Western and Kansas Railroad Company. I'd like to meet with the town officials and talk about a railroad through town and through the valley."

"Just wait," Sam Morlan said, "I'll gather up the men."

He walked down the streets and over to the Lovewell's home; soon he had most of the town fathers in the store. The representative explained his proposition.

"If the towns will buy the bonds we'll build," he said.

There was a long discussion. Some wanted to do it, including Tom and the Morlans. Others said the railroad would build through anyway and it would never miss White Rock. The vote was not to buy the bonds.

"Suit yourselves. We'll build elsewhere."

In 1880 Tom approached the same railroad company with a proposition. "I'll secure land for a right-of-way."

They agreed at once. They platted a town farther west and named it Lovewell's Station, later changing it to Lovewell. They also named the streets after Lovewell family members.

As Lovewell grew, White Rock City began to decline as most businesses moved to the new town. Tom and Orel Jane built a small white house in Lovewell and planned to spend the rest of their lives there. Orel Jane's mother, who had remarried after her husband's death, eventually moved to the valley. She and her second husband, William Scott, a Civil War veteran of H Company, 140th Pennsylvania Regular Infantry, became Tom and Orel Jane's neighbors.

In 1870 the population of Jewell County was 205 persons; by 1875 it had grown to 7,651. The population in the area, which continued to grow, numbered more than 12,000 by 1882. The 1882 census showed 77,635 acres under cultivation. "How's that for fast progress?" Tom said proudly as he quoted the numbers at the new store built by the Morlans in Lovewell.

***

Tom continued to search for his daughters by his first wife, Nancy, but his letters of inquiry always came back negative. One day, after Orel Jane had written Tom's last letter for him and he had nearly given up, the postmaster handed him a letter. It was from his daughter Julaney, who gave a St. Louis address. In it she said: "I have heard of the town of Lovewell in Kansas and wondered if it might in some way be connected with my father. My husband, Edward McCaul, was killed while working at a depot in St. Louis. I am ill, I have six children and am destitute."

Upon reading this news, Tom boarded the first train to St. Louis. There he looked up the address Julaney had given him; at last he had found one of his lost daughters. She was, indeed, destitute: she and her children were in rags, and there was little food in the dilapidated house. After they had greeted each other with hugs and kisses, Tom asked: "Where's your sister?"

"We were adopted by different families and I never saw her again."

"Well, first we'll go uptown and get all of you new clothes and some food. After that I'm taking you home with me."

It took the restaurant a while to fill their empty stomachs. When they had eaten, the family stuffed what belongings they had into a trunk and headed for Tom's home. Orel Jane was equally happy to see her sister's daughter. "Tom, why don't you buy the house across the street for them? I hear it's for sale," She asked.

Tom purchased the house and took care of Julaney and her family until she married John Robinson.

Tom and Orel Jane had two more children of their own, both of whom were born in the valley. Mary Julina was born September 28, 1880, and Diantha Desdimona, September 27, 1883. Tom gave land to each of his children and helped them get started.

***

Later in Tom's life the wanderlust bug struck again. He turned his farming and cattle over to Simpson Grant, and, once again, searched for gold in Wyoming and Colorado, generally without much success.

135

Each time he returned without the "pot of gold at the end of the rainbow", Orel Jane prodded him not to return. "That country was prospected thoroughly many years ago. You're an old man. Why not forget about it? It's just in your blood and you can't get rid of it."

Tom didn't answer. He sat down in his rocking chair and read the latest newspaper, looking for news from a gold field.

Come spring, Tom was sure to pack up, jump on the train and head for another so-called gold field.

Only once did he think he had struck it rich again. He had taken Frank with him to prospect in Colorado, where they were assisted by a Swedish immigrant named Jimmy Svenson, whom Tom had hired in Denver. One day, Svenson was doing the digging while Tom sorted through the rock brought up from a prospect hole. Suddenly Tom jumped up, shouting, "Rich at last, rich at last!"

Svenson came up to see what the excitement was all about. "Just look at this nugget!" He showed it to Jimmy.

"Ya, it sure is a nice nugget. Ay should know. It fell out of my tie clasp."

He held up his tie clasp for Tom to see. Tom was so disgusted he said, "Let's go home."

Despite his failures, Tom's enthusiasm for gold hunting could be quickly rekindled. Not long after returning from his disappointing trip in Colorado, Tom came home with his usual additions to the news of the day. "They've found gold in Alaska," he announced. "Gosh, I guess I'll go."

Orel Jane thought he was joking. (He was seventy-two, while she, sixteen years his junior, was just fifty-six.) "At your age! Surely you don't mean it."

But he did mean it. "I'll take the first train west. I'll pack up right away; I don't want to miss it."

He pulled his carpetbag off the hook and loaded it with the barest necessities. He added his .45 Colt revolver, which he hadn't shot for thirty years, and brought down from the elk antlers his Winchester rifle, which he put in its scabbard. A train whistled in the distance. He gave Orel Jane a quick kiss and ran out the door toward the depot. There was a spring in his gait Orel Jane hadn't noticed for years.

"Good-bye," Orel Jane yelled. "Be sure and write." He turned and waved back. The train was slowing for the depot.

"Just when I thought he was slowing down and ready to spend his final days in his rocking chair. I fear I'll never see him again," Orel Jane said sadly.

She stood in the doorway and watched long after the engine's smoke had disappeared behind the hills. Memories flooded her mind. How many times had she watched him leave to go hunting or guide a trip, wondering if he would return. How many times had she worried that Indian warriors would appear. How many times had she pulled down her trusty rifle and stood it near the door as she studied the hills for signs of trouble or smoke signals. At least she wouldn't worry about Indians this time. She could hear the howl of wolves and coyotes but this time she wouldn't worry if they were real or an Indian imitation. Times had changed and for that she would be forever thankful. This time all she had to worry about was Tom's safe return.

A year later Orel Jane had not heard a word from Tom. It was time again for the Old Settlers Picnic, which was in progress in Babcock Grove. Mrs. Lydia Charles, then president of the Old Settlers Association, was giving her welcoming address.

"However," she concluded. "I'm sorry and I sincerely miss the presence of our friend and friend of all the settlers in the White Rock Valley. I mean the popular, beloved Thomas Lovewell. No word has been received from him and we may never see him alive again. Tales coming out of the Northwest are most disheartening. Many young men have lost their lives…"

She was interrupted by a young man in the huge crowd shouting, "Mrs. Charles, Tom is here by my side. He made it home last evening."

And there he stood, his long white hair falling to his shoulders and his white beard flowing almost to his waist. He stood tall and proud with the same quiet dignity of old. The roar of the crowd shook the treetops in the grove.

Orel Jane made her way through the crowd, threw her arms about him and they hugged each other, just as they had so many years before when the mule ran away on their way home from Junction City.

"What about the gold," she asked at last.

"I found gold all right, but the rascals I had to hire to dig stole it about as fast as we could dig it. I decided it wasn't worth it."

***

Not all of Tom's time was spent hunting treasure. Once a year he and other old-timers met in Kansas City to hash over old times and drink a little liquor. It was the one occasion when Tom forgot his teatotaling habits. One year, after they had eaten dinner at a fancy restaurant, the old-timers returned to the host's place of business, a funeral home. Drinks were passed around as they exchanged stories of the past. Late in the afternoon Tom, not used to hard liquor, passed out. The rest decided to have some fun. They dressed him in funeral attire, laid him in a casket, placed flowers all around him and sat back to see what he would say when he awoke.

Late in the evening Tom wakened, blinked his eyes, then rose and looked around before gleefully announcing, "Whoopee! Resurrection Day and I'm the first man up!"

It was difficult to say when Tom became known as "Old Tom." The term was never used disrespectfully. He was a friend to all settlers and he was never one to provoke to anger.

Old Tom spent his final days in his rocking chair, just sitting there hardly rocking and reminiscing about the good old days, telling and re-telling those stories of years gone by. Children and grandchildren sat around, listening and remembering. Orel Jane continued to keep her notebook handy to record the stories, many of which she was a part.

Tom loved his wife as much as ever and never wanted to be far from her unless he was out looking for gold. If he was reading and didn't want to be disturbed when she came in with the latest gossip or news from the valley, he would say without looking up, "What's that? Who killed the old red hen?" She would flounce back to the kitchen and begin banging pots and kettles. Tom would grin and go back to reading, knowing that by dinner time all would be back to normal. After all, their love and marriage had survived fifty years and more. Together, they had helped settle a beautiful valley and raised a nice family.

Thomas Lovewell often complained of heart trouble over the years, though he lived to be ninety-three. He died March 23,1920, at home. This man, who had fought in the Civil War and saw the white man displace the Indians of the West, had also played an important part in the transition of the beautiful valley in which he lived for fifty-four years.

After complaining of "feeling poorly" earlier in the day, Orel Jane joined Tom on April 16, 1928. She and Tom are buried in White Rock Cemetery, high on a hill east of Lovewell, Kansas.

If they had lived a few more years, Tom and Orel Jane would have seen another great mark of civilization in their favorite valley. A huge earthen dam was constructed near the Rose Hill School. The reservoir draws water from the Republican River and furnishes irrigation water to valley farmers. It is named, appropriately, Lovewell Reservoir. Always pleased to see progress in the area, Tom would have liked this addition to the valley that he loved.

EPILOGUE

Thomas and Orel Jane Lovewell might not have approved of the recent development of White Rock Valley, but today it is still a beautiful, productive place.

Native Americans will never forget the way settlers took their land and plowed under the tall and nutritious switch, Indian and bluestem grasses. It was too beautiful. Tom would have agreed to some extent. The valley was too blessed with life-giving buffalo, deer, antelope and elk. The Lovewells and the Native Americans would miss the fruit of the wild chokecherry and plum bushes; the wild beauty of the roses, goldenrod and other flowers that always broke forth in spring and summer, even Kansas' state flower, the sunflower. They would miss the fish that leapt to the bait when a line was dropped in White Rock Creek, especially Orel Jane, who loved to fish. Today the fish are congregated in Lovewell Lake, where folks languish in boats with lines cast off the side. They probably catch more fish, but it isn't the same.

Tom once sold seed corn through ads in the *White Rock Independent* and, no doubt, he considered it the best quality and the most productive available. He would smile if he could have foreseen the 200-bushel-per-acre corn that farmers produce on the same soil he dug into nearly 150 years ago. It is still as productive as he pronounced it when he camped nearby on his way to Denver. High-quality beef cattle graze the hills that once nurtured the buffalo. The grasses are the same and are well managed for best results.

Lovewell, the only town in this lower part of the valley, is in decline. The large high school, once the valley's pride, sits empty and rotting. The Rose Hill School still stands near Lovewell Lake, a monument to former days. Constructed of native stone, names of former students are carved on outside walls, a sort of directory of bygone days. The seats are still there, with names of students carved on them also. It

140

might be called a museum, but it's more than that—it's living history. Descendants of former students return to view and wonder at the wild roses still blooming nearby, a reminder that Orel Jane and Tom once visited there a century and a half ago.

Small country schools also sit empty. The village itself is still there, albeit with a smaller population and no railroad. Farmsteads, though fewer in number, are well kept, showing their owners' prosperity and pride. When crops need life-giving water it is drawn from Lovewell Lake.

***

Many of the farmers and livestockmen in the area are descendants of the Lovewells and other homesteaders. Other Lovewell descendants moved on to pioneer farther west.

Josephine, Tom and Orel Jane's oldest daughter, married Walter Poole in 1885. His parents, Mr. and Mrs. Abraham Poole, settled in White Rock Valley in 1870, and Josephine and Walter became childhood friends. Walter became a cowboy in Wyoming but later returned to the valley to marry Josephine. Tom and Orel Jane gave them a farm one-half mile west of Lovewell.

Walter was definitely a cow man and a horseman and started his own herds of both. He built a large feed yard near Lovewell and shipped Longhorn cattle from Texas. Sometimes he and other local boys went to Wyoming and rounded up wild horses and trailed them back to Lovewell. There he broke them to either the saddle or the harness, depending on their size, disposition and the market.

Tom enjoyed sitting on the rail fence by the hour and watching Walter rope a wild horse, tie him to a post in the center of the corral and work him out. When the horse was ready Walter mounted and let the horse buck until it quit. Tom often shouted "Ride em' cowboy!" from the corral fence. When Walter got bucked off or was kicked by a fast hoof, Tom laughed and sympathized a bit.

Walter bought land and enlarged his herds. Then in 1908, Walter and Josephine sold out and moved to Texas, where he became a successful rancher. Orel Jane and Tom sure hated to see them go, for they knew they would see little of their grandchildren: Earl, Winnie and Luenette. Josephine's departure meant that the first child born in White Rock Valley would no longer live there.

Grandson James Franklin Lovewell, son of William Frank, born November 18, 1904, whose wife Gloria compiled much of the family history that was drawn from for this book, remembers his grandmother.

"My grandmother was tall for a woman. She never was overweight, remaining slender all her life. In her later years she became almost too thin. Her jaw remained sure and determined. She always wore long dresses that dragged the floor, dark in color with a brightly colored apron and a dark colored kerchief over her head tied under her chin. She had a little severe part right down the middle of her gray hair."

In one of her final chronicles, Orel Jane wrote: "Kansas suits me fine now. But it was only a few year back when we saw Indians riding over the hills—a common sight—but with a worried thought. Friend or foe? Some came with shirts tied around their necks by the sleeves. Others had umbrellas over their heads. Oh, the red gents looked so gay! They all carried spears with strips of blankets—red, white or blue—tied to their spearheads. (This to make folks think they were soldiers of the United States Army). On one spear I noticed a piece of a white lady's scalp— dark hair, long and soft—left by the fence while the owner came looking into our house. You never closed a door on an Indian unless you were looking for trouble. I went out and examined the spear with the scalp on it; the lady no doubt had been a victim of the noble Red Man.

"Let's thank the pioneers who, with God's help, subdued the wilds and, by their courage and bravery, assured us a home in this beautiful valley of White Rock. Let us be thankful we can lie down and sleep without fear. It seemed but yesterday when the buffalo came to get water and tramped the potatoes out of the ground. We saw such vast herds that the ground fairly trembled under their hooves.

"My husband was a generous man. Many a settler and his family spent their first night at our cabin. Then he would take them out and find the best locations for a homestead. He would teach them to watch out for Indians and how to shoot a rifle, something most of them had little experience with before."

Like Orel Jane, Tom's grandchildren also remembered him fondly. Grandson James Franklin Lovewell recalls: "Granddad was a staunch Republican and was actively interested in politics all of his life. On one particular occasion he, along with Grant, Steve and I, attended a political caucus to select a candidate to run for some office. Old Tom differed with another person in attendance—a much younger man. He said to Granddad, 'If it weren't for your white hair I'd hit you right on top of you head,' to which Granddad replied, 'Don't let my white hair stop you, young man.' The man made a rush at Granddad and when he got within reach Granddad flung him clear over his head. The fellow sailed through the air, landing against the far wall, completely dazed." Most people there didn't know that Tom had been a wrestler once and that this was one of his favorite tricks used to win matches.

***

Native Americans rarely cross the valley anymore, but if they did, they might chance on a large museum that represents a Pawnee chief's hogan on the hill to the south. The Kansas State Historical Society scraped away the thin layer of earth that covered the floor of his hogan, exposing primitive tools, toasted corn, and a cistern that served as storage for buffalo meat. In the rear is the traditional buffalo skull that was the center of every worship service before beginning a hunt or a prayer for success in stealing horses.

It's fascinating to drive through the valley and contemplate the dangerous life once lived here by the Lovewells and all other early day settlers' to visualize buffalo and other wild animals grazing on grass that was nearly as high as the hump of the tallest bull buffalo. One can almost imagine Orel Jane standing in the doorway of their cabin watching nervously as Tom drove off to hunt game or to guide another settlers' train. One can see her surveying the landscape, gun in hand, seeking the slightest hint that Indians might be approaching and, if so, wondering whether they meant trouble or merely sought another slice of her homemade bread. Round Mound, where Indians came to view the valley and Orel Jane scanned for signs of trouble each day, still stands.

Black Morgan's spirit still watches over the valley. When he grew old, Tom, true to his word, never sold him but put him out to pasture, never to be ridden again. When he became stoved up and his teeth grew too bad for grazing grass, Tom kept him near the barn and fed him oats. One day Tom came out with a bucket of oats to find Black Morgan breathing his last. He called Orel Jane and they just stood there gazing at the faithful stallion that had sired so many colts. He had saved Tom's life once or twice and had carried him many miles. Tom and the boys slid him onto a stone boat and buried him on a hill overlooking White Rock Valley. Simpson Grant thought he saw a tear in his father's eye as he dumped in the last shovelful of dirt.

"Both of us are the last of the frontier breed," Tom said, then slowly walked away.

THE END

About the Author

Roy Alleman was born and raised on a livestock farm in north central Nebraska. He graduated from Wiggle Creek High School, a consolidated high school south of Loup City, Nebraska, and attended the University of Nebraska and Hastings College. He farmed early in life but later turned to journalism as a career. He has served as the editor of the *Central Nebraska Farmer-Stockman* of Cozad, the *Custer County Chief* in Broken Bow, and as farm editor of the *Hastings Tribune*, all in Nebraska. He is the author of the popular book *Blizzard 1949*, which chronicles the terrible blizzards and deep snows of one Nebraska winter. Roy passed away December 1999 at the age of 90. His wife, Irene, currently resides in Grand Island, Nebraska.

CPSIA information can be obtained at www.ICGtesting.com
Printed in the USA
268813BV00001B/81/A